PEGGY OVERBECK

THE SHAMAN'S GIFT

Black Rose Writing | Texas

ISBN: 978-1-68513-018-3
PUBLISHED BY BLACK ROSE WRITING
www.blackrosewriting.com

Printed in the United States of America
Suggested Retail Price (SRP) $18.95

The Shaman's Gift is printed in EB Garamond

*As a planet-friendly publisher, Black Rose Writing does its best to eliminate unnecessary waste to reduce paper usage and energy costs, while never compromising the reading experience. As a result, the final word count vs. page count may not meet common expectations.

Author photograph by Ravette Photography, Inc

Dedicated to Barbara J. Lowes

Special thanks to my editor, Cindy Vangilder, and also to C. J. Larkin and Robert Lowes for their continued support and encouragement.

THE
SHAMAN'S
GIFT

I

A full moon illuminated the warm Texas evening. Emily Henderson walked out of the West-End Steakhouse and paused at the entrance while she rummaged in her purse for car keys. She wore a conservative business suit, yet with her long hair pulled into a ponytail and the smattering of freckles sprinkled across her nose, she looked more like a little girl playing dress-up than a businesswoman.

The West-End teemed with people winding down after their workweek. The renovated area, meant to rejuvenate downtown after dark, was two blocks long, with a cluster of inviting restaurants and clubs.

Emily exited the area, crossed Elm Street at Lamar, and continued to Main Street. Though just a few blocks away from the thriving West-End, trash blew down the deserted street like tumbleweeds rolling through a ghost town.

Dan disapproved of her going alone to her firm's annual dinner party. She argued it was being held at the West-End Steakhouse, hosted by the company president, and as a new employee, she should at least make an appearance.

Dan had been invited, but he reminded Emily he never missed the opening day of dove season. He finally agreed to let her go alone.

Emily felt a little guilty about having such a good time without him. Everyone urged her to stay on after dinner, but she wanted to get home and call Dan at the cabin so he wouldn't worry.

The parking lot next to her office was empty except for her old Buick convertible, which was in dire need of a new top. Thankfully, the motor turned over.

Emily bypassed the entrance to I-35, heading instead for Harry Hines Boulevard. If Dan were with her, he would chide her for being intimidated by freeways. She would conquer her fear of freeways eventually, though not tonight.

In the shadows of a side street, two men slouched in a nondescript brown car. As Emily passed, the car pulled out behind her and followed at a distance.

Emily swung onto Harry Hines and headed north. She waited at the stoplight in front of Parkland Hospital as a throng of men and women, some clad in blue, others in green, crossed the street from the employees' parking lot to the hospital entrance to begin their shift. The emergency room would be packed tonight, as it was every night.

She admired people who constantly ministered to what some cold-hearted people called the dregs of society. People who were hurt, without a doctor affiliated with a hospital, many without insurance, most without money to pay—all came to Parkland.

Emily waited at the light to cross Walnut Hill Lane, which was supposedly the dividing line between the wet and dry areas of the City. South of Walnut Hill, liquor-by-the-drink was sold.

North of Walnut Hill was supposed to be dry. However, restaurant and club owners got around the law by making their establishments "private clubs."

Mexican restaurants and clubs gave way farther north to country-western bars and topless places. Emily heard music coming from a club as she passed. Though it was not the safest stretch of Harry Hines to travel at night, it was the shortest route home except for the freeway.

A siren screamed directly behind her. Startled, she glanced in her rearview mirror. A light flashed atop the roof of a brown car—certainly not a police car. She frowned as she looked for a place to pull over to let it pass. Casa Miguel was on her right. She turned into the parking lot.

The brown car pulled in behind her and stopped.

A man in the passenger seat reached out the window to remove the red light from the roof of the car. The siren was silent. She watched in her rearview mirror as an older, heavy-set man stepped from behind the wheel and started toward her. Gray sideburns stuck out from a Dallas Cowboys cap tilted low over his forehead.

He stopped outside her door. She lowered her window and looked up into hard eyes, a full-lipped cruel mouth, and a nose covered with broken capillaries.

"Step out of the car, ma'am," he said.

Emily hesitated. "Who are you? May I see some identification, please?"

He reached into his pocket and held out his badge.

She looked at it carefully. "What's the problem, officer?"

"Just step out of the car, ma'am."

Emily grabbed her purse and got out, stumbling in her haste. The officer caught her arm and kept her from falling.

"Driver's license?" he snapped.

Her hand shook as she gave it to him.

He peered at the picture on the license, then back at her.

"We're part of a special task force cracking down on drunk drivers, Mrs. Henderson. Your car was weaving all over the road."

"I—I only had one glass of wine with dinner, officer. I'm certainly not drunk." She chastised herself for admitting she had anything to drink.

"It's a good thing you didn't lie to me. I can smell it on you. Wait right here."

He walked back to his car, talked with his partner for several minutes, then slowly returned.

Emily unconsciously crossed her arms across her breasts as his eyes moved over her body and back to her face. He gave her a smile from between closed lips.

"Well, guess what? Our computer shows an outstanding warrant for your arrest. Now, what do ya know about that?"

Emily's eyes widened. "There must be some mistake."

He scratched the back of his neck. "Lady, I'd hate to tell you how many times I've heard that. Park your car and lock it." He glanced down at her left hand. "Maybe your husband can pick it up later after he bails you out."

"He's out of town," Emily replied and immediately regretted it. What was the matter with her?

He didn't seem to notice. "What we're gonna do is head downtown and see about that warrant."

A young man stepped from the car and held the front passenger door for her. He was of medium height, muscular, with white-blond hair. His face was expressionless, yet he managed to frighten her without saying a word. She noticed the military creases of his shirt because Dan insisted she iron his shirts the same way.

"Don't you want me to get into the back seat?" she asked.

"No. We have some equipment back there," the young man replied.

The older officer smirked. "Maybe you can get somebody to bail you out before your husband gets back and finds out you've been bad."

Emily tried to keep the frustration out of her voice. "I told you there's been some kind of mix-up. I've never had a ticket in my life."

"Yeah, sure, lady. The computer made a mistake."

As they entered I-35 heading south, she gripped her folded arms. God, she hated freeways.

"What are your names, officer?"

"I'm Officer Hunter." The older man nodded toward the back seat. "That there's Officer Barnes."

They continued in silence as Emily watched the road.

She jerked upright in her seat when they passed the exit to the Sterrett Justice Center and moved onto Interstate 30 toward Fort Worth. "You've missed our exit. Where are you going?"

Barnes leaned forward. Emily felt his breath on her cheek. He placed one hand on her shoulder. The barrel of a .38 special pressed against the side of her neck.

She had always heard the expression "cold steel." It wasn't true. The metal burned into her skin.

"Just sit nice and quiet and enjoy the ride," Barnes said.

Emily's voice quivered when she could finally speak. "Where are you taking me?"

Hunter turned to her with his version of a smile. "Just a quick detour."

Her right hand inched toward the door handle. Officer Barnes tapped her cheek with his gun. "Uh, uh."

As they turned off I-30, Emily fought hysteria. She must try to think. Her chance of escape would come when the car stopped. She must be ready.

Hunter turned onto a two-lane blacktop road. He drove a short way, then pulled onto a narrow lane. They came to a stop in a clearing hidden from the road by trees and thick underbrush. At the end of the clearing was some sort of ravine.

Barnes opened Emily's door and motioned her outside with the .38. She sat frozen, unable to move.

Hunter came around the car. "Come on," he snarled, "get out!"

Emily shrank back into the seat. He pulled her out of the car and shoved her to the ground as Barnes holstered his gun.

"Please, please don't hurt me," Emily cried.

Her eyes darted from Hunter to Barnes. Her fear was replaced by blazing anger. "You must be out of your minds. My God, this is kidnapping!"

Hunter grabbed Emily's ponytail and twisted it around his hand. She cried out as he gave a hard jerk, pulling her to her feet.

Emily lunged at him. Her long fingernails searched for his eyes. He caught her hand. "You bitch," he yelled. His burly fist smashed into her nose. Emily dropped to the ground. Blood ran down onto her mouth and chin.

Hunter nodded toward her. "How 'bout it Barnes, you wanna go first?"

Barnes' lip curled as he eyed the blood on Emily's face. "No thanks. Come on, Hunter. Let's just get the job done and get back to town."

Maybe now was her chance. Emily half ran, half crawled toward the ravine. She was almost there when Barnes caught her. She screamed as he viciously kicked her in the ribs again and again.

He smiled down at her. "Don't be in such a hurry. You'll be going for a swim soon enough."

Hunter started toward her. Emily looked up to see a vision of an Indian woman. A voice within her said if there was any chance of escape, it would have to be now. With strength born of the instinct to survive, Emily rose to a crouch and stumbled toward the ravine, almost reaching it before Hunter spotted her.

He swore, drew his gun, and fired, barely missing her.

As she turned to look back, the voice told her to turn her head to the right--a move that saved her life. Hunter's second shot only grazed her left temple.

Emily tumbled into the ravine and landed waist-deep in the river.

Hunter saw her head jerk on impact and heard the splash as she hit the water. As he started toward the ravine to make sure she was dead, a car's headlights shone through the brush as it passed the clearing.

Hunter swore as he got back into the car and waited. The intruder continued only a short way before pulling off the road.

He turned to Barnes. "It's too risky to crawl down the ravine now. Besides, I'm positive the bitch is dead."

Barnes nodded agreement, pulled his hat down over his eyes, and propped his knees on the dashboard.

Hunter started the car and drove carefully, with the lights off, until they reached the blacktop road.

. . . . .

In the pre-dawn silence, Emily laid against the scrubby bush that had broken her fall, and kept her from drowning. From some hidden reservoir, she found the strength to pull herself out of the water, and claw her way up the ravine onto solid ground. She moved a hand across her blood-dried mouth. Mud was caked over the wound to her temple. The side of her face felt numb. Every breath caused excruciating pain in her ribs.

Emily closed her eyes for a moment, then opened them again. Though terrified of what she might find, her eyes darted around the clearing like an animal searching for predators. The clearing was empty.

Emily struggled to stand. Her legs wouldn't support her. She fell back onto the ground, then began to crawl. It seemed to take forever to cross the clearing, for she had to stop and rest every few minutes. At last, she made it onto the gravel road.

Exhausted, she laid back as blackness overtook her again. Her body shook from shock and her wet clothes.

The sun had moved over the horizon when Emily woke up again. If she were to survive, she must reach the blacktop road—and help. It no longer mattered how much it hurt to breathe.

She would not die here. She began to crawl again. After what seemed like hours, she felt the smooth surface of the blacktop road beneath her bloody outstretched hands.

She started to pass out again. A primeval animal growl escaped from her throat as, with the last of her strength, she rolled into the middle of the road and lay still.

A vintage Chevrolet pickup truck moved slowly toward the city. It's bed was packed with an assortment of vegetables for the farmers' market. The elderly couple always looked forward to their weekly outing, seeing good friends who had bought their produce for years.

Brakes squealed as the truck came to a halt a few feet from Emily's body. The man jumped out of the truck and hurried to the young woman. Emily's eyes opened, wild with fear. She tried to scream. No sound came out.

The old woman hurried from the truck, sat down in the road, and gently put her arms around Emily, who babbled incoherently through swollen lips.

"We need to get you to the hospital. Can you stand for us to lift you?" Emily nodded slowly, her eyes never leaving the woman's face.

The old couple gently carried her to the truck and lifted her inside. The man handed his wife a blanket from the back. Together, they removed her wet clothes. The woman wrapped the blanket around Emily, who succumbed to its warmth.

2

Clarice Weitzel jerked awake to the shrill ringing of the telephone. She glanced at the clock radio—eight a.m. It felt like the middle of the damned night. She took a breath to settle her jangled nerves and grabbed the phone.

"It's your nickel," she growled.

"Good morning to you, too," Nurse Janet Walker replied.

Clarice sat up, now wide awake. Her friend was on duty at Parkland Hospital. She would not be calling unless there was a problem.

"Sorry to wake you. They brought a young woman named Emily Henderson into Emergency early this morning. She had been beaten and shot in the head. Dr. Asher used locals during the procedures because of the concussion possibility, although Emily said the attack was early last evening."

"Emily said the men responsible were police officers Hunter and Barnes. I phoned Lt. Bannister then tried you at the Center. I knew you would want to know."

"Be there as soon as I brush my teeth. Sorry to be so grumpy. Didn't get home from the Center until five. Sleep deprivation has become a way of life."

Janet laughed. "By the way, it's raining cats and dogs. Be sure to wear the yellow rain slicker that Bannister gave you for your birthday."

Clarice strode down the hospital corridor, removing her rain slicker as she went. Her silver hair was cut in a wash-and-wear pixie, which complemented a tanned face devoid of makeup. Tall and rawboned, her pale blue eyes looked out at the world with a no-nonsense expression.

She handed Janet a box of doughnuts and paper cups of steaming coffee. "Peace offering for you. Breakfast for me. The stuff you call coffee tastes like something unmentionable."

Clarice chuckled. "Bannister and I still have the money thing going on. I agreed to cough up a dollar each time I use profanity or 'dirty words', so I'm watching my mouth."

Janet smiled as she bit into her doughnut. "I love these—apology accepted. Bannister is around here someplace."

"Tell me about our patient?" Clarice asked.

"She's in la-la land, thanks to morphine." Janet shook her head. "Lord knows she needs it. A bullet wound that luckily just grazed her temple, three broken ribs, broken nose, lacerations of the legs and hands, and two very black eyes."

"Wow. How about her mental condition?"

"She was in shock when an old couple found her and brought her in. She seemed perfectly calm. Kept talking about a traffic ticket. Dr. Asher is concerned about post-traumatic stress disorder."

"It wouldn't be surprising after what she's been through," Clarice said as she grabbed one of the coffee containers and two doughnuts. "I'll sit with her for a while. What's her room number?"

"104. Though she will probably be out for another hour."

"I'll try to find Lou." Clarice spun around, almost knocking the unlit cigar from the mouth of a stocky man in a rumpled suit.

"Ah, Clarice, my love. I was wondering when you would show up." Lou Bannister's wide smile lit up an otherwise brooding face.

"Hi, Lou. Looks like we're back together again," Clarice said.

"Yeah. I've missed you." He cleared his throat. "You gonna share the coffee and one of those doughnuts?"

"I ain't gonna share jack—a damned thing with you, flatfoot. Get your own doughnut and keep your mitts off my coffee. The hospital junk is good enough for you."

"I love it when you talk tough to me. The 'damned' makes $9.00 you owe me. When you hit $20.00, you can take me out to dinner," he said, snatching one of her doughnuts. "They found Mrs. Henderson in the middle of Farm-To-Market 84. I sent a couple of guys back with the old man to pinpoint the exact location."

He took a sip of her coffee. "Um. Good. Dr. Asher and I have been discussing the case. She was not raped, so there was nothing to give us any DNA. I'm hoping my boys find some evidence at the crime scene."

"What about the two cops?"

"We're running them through the computer. I'll be talking to them later today."

She smiled. "You're one step ahead, as always. I'll go sit with Emily. She shouldn't be alone when she wakes up."

"I'll be around. Let me know when she comes to."

• • • • • •

Clarice stared at Emily's swollen and discolored face. A large bandage covered her left temple.

Janet entered the room and put her arm around Clarice's shoulder. "With her long brown hair spread over the pillow like that, she kind of reminds you of Laurie, doesn't she?"

Clarice wiped her eyes with the back of her hand. "Yeah. But then, they all do." She dropped onto the chair next to the bed and closed her eyes as Janet left the room.

After some time, Emily's eyes fluttered open. The window blinds were drawn, yet her eyes still hurt in the dim light. She cautiously glanced around the room and stopped at the woman dozing in the chair next to her bed.

"Who are you?" she whispered at last. The act of opening her mouth made her head throb.

Clarice woke with a start. "Oh. I'm Clarice Weitzel from the Women's Crisis Center."

Emily closed her eyes again and groaned. "My head is going to explode."

"Want me to call your nurse?"

"Uh-huh. Is my husband here?"

"No. We didn't know how to reach him. You were asleep—thanks to drugs. We didn't know his first name, and you weren't in the phone book."

"It's Dan."

"How can we reach him?"

"If today is Saturday, he should be at the cabin."

Emily touched the bandage on her temple as though trying to remember what it was doing there.

"Is there a phone?" Clarice asked as she reached over and brushed the hair from Emily's damp forehead.

Emily flinched and turned away. "214-555-1987. The cabin is just this side of Canton."

"Do you want me to call him?"

"Uh-huh. It's a cell phone. It'll find him."

"I'll go call and let Nurse Walker know you need something for pain."

Clarice found Janet at the nurses' station. "Emily's awake, though probably not for long if you have any more joy juice. She's in a lot of pain. She asked me to call her husband."

"I'll take care of the morphine. You can use the phone in the nurses' lounge."

"Okay. Would you tell Lou that Emily's awake?"

"Sure."

• • • • •

Clarice was about to hang up when someone picked up the telephone. "Is this Dan Henderson?" she asked.

"Yeah. Who is this?"

"Mr. Henderson, my name is Clarice Weitzel. I'm calling from Parkland Hospital. Your wife, Emily, is here."

"Emily? What's wrong? What's happened?"

"I'm sorry. She's been in the emergency room since early this morning. We didn't know how to reach you until now."

"What do you mean? Was she in an accident? Is she badly hurt?"

"Dr. Asher will explain everything when you get here. Emily's doing okay. She may be in the hospital for a day or two. Come to the third-floor east nurses' station and ask for Nurse Janet Walker. She will notify Dr. Asher that you are here. I am with the Women's Crisis Center. I'll stay with Emily until you arrive."

"I would like some answers now, but it looks like I will not get any."

"I'm sorry, Mr. Henderson, I am not allowed to discuss your wife's condition."

"Are you sure I can't speak with Emily?"

"They gave her a shot for pain and she's asleep."

· · · · ·

Emily looked up as Clarice returned to her room.

"Did you talk to him?"

Clarice nodded. "He asked to speak to you. I wasn't sure you were up to it."

Emily tried to smile. She winced instead. "Thanks. How did you know?"

"I've been working with women in crisis for the past five years," Clarice said.

"I heard Dr. Asher say I'm lucky to be alive. I'm not so sure." She turned her head away. "Dan didn't want me to go to the dinner. What if I hadn't?" Emily's voice trailed off.

"Hush. I know you are hurting, physically and mentally. You will get through this, Emily."

"You don't know Dan. How am I going to face him?"

"Is there anything you want to talk to me about?"

Emily turned her head away. "No, not now."

Clarice changed the subject. "Did Janet bring your pain medication?"

"Yes. Though it only helps with the physical pain."

"Dr. Asher is right. You are very lucky to be alive. Make it enough for now. The rest will come later when you get well."

Emily closed her eyes. She was suddenly sleepy. The morphine at last brought temporary escape.

$\bullet \quad \bullet \quad \bullet \quad \bullet \quad \bullet$

Later that afternoon, Clarice caught up with Bannister in the hall. "They gave her another shot, and she's been sleeping. I need caffeine." She touched his arm. "Hold on a minute. This has to be him."

They watched a man stroll into the waiting room, then move on to the nurses' station. He wore a designer western shirt with military creases, immaculate boot-cut jeans, and expensive lizard cowboy boots.

Clarice glanced at Bannister, her expression betraying her distaste. "It's after five o'clock. It's only about a two-hour drive from Canton," she said as they approached the desk. "I wonder what took our Mr. Henderson so long? Looks like he took time to change clothes and fluff up before bothering to come and see about his wife."

Bannister did not reply.

Clarice took a deep breath as they reached Dan and forced a smile. "Mr. Henderson?"

"Right. You the lady who called?"

She nodded. "Clarice Weitzel. This gentleman is Lieutenant Louis Bannister of the police department. We wondered whether you were still in Canton. Dove hunting must have been pretty good?"

Dan nodded to Bannister, then turned back to Clarice, ignoring her comments. "How is my wife?"

"Dr. Asher should be here momentarily. Wait, here he is now."

She introduced the two men. Dr. Asher extended his hand. "Mr. Henderson, I see the waiting room's empty. Let's talk in there."

Clarice and Bannister waited at the nurses' station. They watched Dan's expression through the glass as Dr. Asher spoke. They knew the moment Dr. Asher told him about Emily's injuries.

Dan's face tightened. He looked more angry than upset.

"I wonder if his anger is directed toward the men who kidnapped his wife or toward Emily?" Clarice mused.

Dan Henderson rose abruptly and started out of the waiting room. Dr. Asher—looking puzzled—followed along, still talking to him. Dan moved toward the nurses' station.

Clarice and Bannister couldn't help overhearing the one-sided conversation. "Mr. Henderson," Dr. Asher continued, "your wife is in an extremely fragile mental condition. Though she may seem fine to you, she is suffering from post-traumatic stress disorder."

Dan looked more annoyed than interested in what Dr. Asher had to say.

"Mr. Henderson, I do not believe your wife's mind is ready to cope with what she has experienced. I cannot emphasize strongly enough that she begins immediate treatment with a therapist. She needs help to reduce the damage of her experience. There are several excellent psychiatrists who both Mrs. Weitzel and I can recommend."

"Thank you, doctor," Dan said. He turned to Clarice, clearly dismissing Dr. Asher. "What's Emily's room number again?"

"104. Before you go in, please understand..."

Dan ignored her and started down the hall.

Bannister put a hand on his shoulder. "Mr. Henderson, I wonder if we can have a few words after you visit with your wife? We'll be in the waiting room."

"Okay, Lieutenant." He disappeared into Emily's room.

Bannister sighed. "So that's the husband."

"Yeah. Real pretty, ain't he?" Clarice replied.

3

Dan stopped by the foot of Emily's bed. She'd heard him come in and could feel him staring at her. She couldn't muster the courage to open her eyes.

"You awake, Emily?" he asked after several minutes.

The irritation in his voice was unmistakable. She'd heard the tone often enough. Emily had learned to pay close attention to the tone of a person's voice because it often revealed much more than what they were saying.

She opened her eyes and tried to smile. "I'm so glad you're here."

He moved to the chair next to her bed. He didn't kiss her or even touch her hand. Perhaps, she thought, he was afraid of catching something.

"I leave town for one night and you end up in the hospital."

His tone gave no hint of compassion or love, only accusation.

Emily did not reply.

Dan leaned toward her but avoided looking at her face. "You don't have to be afraid to admit who really did this. It's okay. You can tell me the truth."

Stunned, she shrank from him. "I *am* telling the truth!"

He uttered a long sigh as he sat back in his chair.

With Dan no longer looming over her, some of the tension left her body. "I left the party early to come home and call you at the cabin. I was driving up Harry Hines when two policemen pulled me over."

Hunter's and Barnes' faces flashed before her. She willed herself to continue. "They were in an unmarked brown car with a siren and a red light whirring just like a police car. They said they were working undercover. I demanded to see their badges, and they showed them to me. They were Officers Hunter and Barnes."

"Okay. Go on."

Emily closed her eyes. She did not want to see his expression. "The older one came to my car, took my license, and returned to their car. A few minutes later, he came back. He said I had an outstanding arrest warrant. They gave me no choice except to drive downtown with them."

"So you just got into their car--just like that?"

Emily's voice quivered. "What else could I do?"

"What happened then?"

Her mouth was dry. She grimaced as she licked her cracked lips. "Could you hand me the glass of ice chips?" She caught him staring at her mouth with revulsion. "I realized something was wrong when we bypassed the Sterrett Justice exit."

Dan's voice dripped with sarcasm. "So you finally figured out something was wrong?"

Emily flinched. She could not believe how Dan was acting. "I don't want to talk anymore." Her anger suddenly flared. "Do I have to describe all the details?"

Dan began to pace. Emily wondered if he thought she was lying or just stupid? Surely, he realized, if she were going to lie, she was intelligent enough to think up a better story. He probably thought she was lying and stupid.

Dan's back was turned to her. "You're right. I don't need to hear all the gory details." He walked out of her room without even a goodbye.

If he intended to punish her, it didn't work this time. Emily was too full of anger and pride. Anger for allowing him to bully her in the past, and pride because she stood up to him today. Her body rocked, and she started to rub her arms. She held herself as she curled into a fetal position, knowing she'd have to face him again tomorrow.

Dan approached Janet at the nurses' station. "I believe Dr. Asher said Emily could go home tomorrow. What time will she be released?"

"Sometime after eleven o'clock. Dr. Asher usually finishes rounds by then."

"That'll work. Tell her I will be here after church—about one o'clock."

Bannister and Clarice stood nearby and caught the exchange. They looked at each other. So Dan was leaving already.

"Got a minute Mr. Henderson?" Bannister called out. "This won't take long. The waiting room is still empty. We can talk in there."

Clarice followed them.

"Why is she coming?" Dan asked.

"Mrs. Weitzel heads the Women's Crisis Center. She works with the hospital and police in these types of situations."

They settled at a table. Bannister leaned back in his chair. "Why don't you give us a little background about you and your wife?"

"Not much to tell. Emily was eighteen when we met at church in Abilene. We'd been dating about a year when her grandmother passed away. Emily was alone and overwhelmed, so I decided we should get married. That was about a year and a half ago. My company, The Harmon Group, transferred me. We've been living here for the past six months."

"Let's talk about last night. I understand Mrs. Henderson attended a company function, and you were out of town."

"That's right. She works at Becker Insurance Company. It was their annual office party. Emily felt she should go. Against my better judgment, I allowed her to attend."

A smile played on Lou's mouth as he stole a glance at Clarice's scarlet face.

"Why didn't you go with her?" he asked.

Dan smiled. "I have not missed the opening day of dove season in ten years."

"I see," Lou replied. "Please go on."

"It's hard to believe two policemen kidnapped Emily." He shrugged his shoulders. "When I saw her just now, she told me about leaving the dinner, the police stopping her, and being forced to ride downtown in their car. She didn't want to talk about her injuries."

"I get the impression you think she's lying," Bannister said.

"Well, come on, you have to admit her story is pretty far-fetched."

Bannister tried not to show his irritation. "There *are* two policemen named Hunter and Barnes. They are partners out of the precinct which covers the area of Harry Hines Boulevard that Mrs. Henderson described. Why do you think your wife would make up a story that could so easily be checked?"

"I do not know. I'll be taking her home tomorrow. I will eventually get the complete story. She is just too ashamed to tell me now."

Clarice's control disappeared. "Ashamed! Mr. Henderson, your young wife has been through a horrific trauma less than twenty-four hours ago. She is emotionally fragile. Dr. Asher is concerned about post-traumatic stress disorder. Emily narrowly escaped being killed. The bandage on her head covers a gunshot wound. Does her condition not mean anything to you?" She was so angry she couldn't continue.

"Someone has apprised me of Emily's condition, Ms. Weitzel," Dan snapped.

"I am waiting until tomorrow to get a statement from your wife because I don't want to push her." Bannister's eyes narrowed. "I think it would be a bad idea for anyone to push her right now about anything, don't you, Mr. Henderson?"

Bannister's expression suggested it would not be smart for Dan to reply. "Someone attempted to murder your wife, Mr. Henderson, and I intend to find out who and why."

Dan smirked. "Maybe she picked up some guy on Harry Hines after the party and things got out of hand."

Bannister frowned. "Has your wife ever given you reason to suspect she is playing around?"

"Just suspicion. I am not the first man to be taken in by a seemingly helpless girl with a sweet face." He stood up. "If that's all, Lieutenant, I need to get going."

"I'll be talking with Mrs. Henderson around noon tomorrow if you would care to be here. I intend to interview officers Hunter and Barnes later this evening."

"No thanks. You can fill me in later if you learn anything you think I should know."

Clarice exploded as soon as the door closed. "What a scumbag! He doesn't give a tinker's damn about her. Damned sanctimonious bastard."

"No charge for the bill you just ran up, since I agree with you. Of course, at this point, we know little about Emily Henderson. Dan may have reason to believe she is lying, which he doesn't care to share with us—but somehow I doubt it."

• • •

"I am not asleep—just thinking," Emily said as Clarice slid into the chair next to her bed.

"Lt. Bannister and I caught up with Dan before he left the hospital."

"He made it clear he thinks I'm lying. I don't believe I should have to try to convince him I'm telling the truth, do you?"

"Of course not. Dr. Asher will probably release you tomorrow. Dan will be here about one o'clock—after church. Lt. Bannister plans to talk with you around noon."

"Dan won't be here? Thank God! Do you think Lt. Bannister will be able to prove I'm telling the truth?"

"I certainly hope so. There's not very much to go on. Lou has people at the crime scene searching for evidence. He's interviewing Hunter and Barnes tonight. Lou Bannister is a damned good cop. I've worked with him for five years. You can trust him to keep digging until he gets to the bottom of this."

"I am so glad he's waiting until tomorrow to talk to me. I could handle nothing more today." She sank back onto the pillows. Her eyelids began to droop. "I think I need to be by myself for a while. I can hardly keep my eyes open."

"Sure, I understand." Clarice walked to the nightstand as she reached into her purse. "Here is my business card. My home phone number is on the back. Also, Janet and the night nurse know how to reach me. Call me if you need anything at all—any time—day or night. Now try to get some sleep, young lady." Clarice turned to leave.

"I'd like you to be here tomorrow when I talk to Lt. Bannister," Emily said.

Clarice smiled and patted her shoulder. "Sure. Whatever you want." She picked up her rain slicker and left the room.

After Clarice had gone, Emily tried to think, but a wall surrounded her mind which she could not climb over. Something important continued to elude her. Maybe her mind would become clear after she slept. She curled up into a fetal position, wrapping her arms around her body for protection. Somehow, she would stop Hunter and Barnes from getting away with destroying her life.

4

Philip Barnes admired his newly sun-streaked hair in the bedroom mirror as he read the note from his roommate. He wore skin-tight jeans and a black tee-shirt which showed off his muscular, weight-trained body. Nancy was complaining—as usual—that he didn't give her enough attention. What she meant was he had not "made love to her" as she liked to put it, in at least two days.

His mouth pursed in irritation as he held the note to his nose, made a face at the perfumed parchment, and tossed it in the trash.

He grabbed the phone. His voice was soft when he spoke.

"Hey, babe, how's your day going?"

Nancy Osborne, owner and operator of The Treasure Trove, stood in her store's workshop, in the midst of what at first glance appeared to be an assortment of junk, but was, in fact, valuable antiques in various stages of repair.

She brushed a wisp of fly-away blond hair from her forehead with tapered piano-player fingers. The skin on her face was taunt, almost translucent, over high hollowed cheekbones. Long, delicate arms and legs reached out of a model-thin body.

"So, so, I suppose," she replied.

Philip continued, as though he didn't notice her icy tone. "I got your note. I'm off tonight. Why don't we go out?"

Nancy smiled to herself. She had already heard about his trouble at work through her vast pipeline. If he was taking her out, he obviously wanted her to do something for him, probably supply an alibi. It would not be the first time.

Her voice was a husky promise. "I'll think of something very special to show how much I've missed you. Let's start off at Hoffbrau. I know how you love their steaks."

Having dinner at his favorite restaurant was guaranteed to put him in an amorous mood. "I also got some new weed."

"Sounds like a party. See you about seven."

Philip hung up the phone, then picked it up again.

"Señora Lambert, por favor."

"Who calls?"

"Her brother."

There was a moment's hesitation on the other end of the line. "The Senora, she no here."

"Thanks a lot." Barnes slammed down the receiver and headed for the front door. The living room was filled to suffocation with expensive antique furniture. Nancy said it was worth a bundle, but as far as he was concerned, it was just so much junk. He grabbed his jacket from the hall closet and left the house, slamming the lacquered red door behind him.

Outside, workmen were installing stained-glass windows. Another crew had started enclosing the side porch. He would never understand why Nancy wanted to waste good money on this old house. A high-rise apartment like Taylor's was more like it. Well, he'd be out of this claustrophobic dump soon enough.

Barnes looked with pride at the black Corvette parked at the curb before sliding behind the wheel. The Vette was his only love. He turned the key and caressed the shift knob as the engine roared into life. Now this was something worth spending money on. He raced down the street, stopped at the light, then revved the engine. He listened with pleasure to the sound of the pipes as he took off again.

Just a few short blocks away, the homes became massive, with manicured lawns and an array of sprinklers preserving the St. Augustine grass. Branches of the old trees entwined high over the center of the streets, sun filtering softly through the leaves, giving an air of serenity to the morning. Philip briefly wondered what it must be like to live here in this world of money, but decided the price would be much too high.

Turning into a wide circular driveway, he stopped in front of a two-story Georgian house. Philip walked to the front door and leaned on the bell. A Mexican woman of indeterminate age answered.

"Señora Lambert, por favor," Philip said.

"Señora Lambert not at home."

He ignored her comment. "Tell Señora Lambert her brother is here."

"No comprende English, senor."

"Like hell you don't." Philip pushed past her and headed for the home's living room, leaving the maid to trail along behind him.

Marcia Lambert heard the voices, yet continued reading her book.

Philip sauntered into the living room and stood glowering down at her.

Without acknowledging his presence, she set her book aside, moved gracefully to the sideboard, and poured herself a drink.

Marcia Lambert was a beautiful woman in her mid-thirties. She was as tall as Philip—his exact twin. Her perfectly streaked blond hair fell onto tanned shoulders. Only the wariness in her green eyes belied the serenity of her finely featured face.

After dismissing the maid, she turned to face him. Her eyes narrowed as she appraised him with a look of utter disdain.

"Okay. What do you want?"

He smiled slowly. "Now, Martha, is this any way to talk to your brother?"

"My name is Marcia," she snapped.

Philip shrugged. "Sorry. I forgot. When you wouldn't talk on the phone, and with your new husband on the golf course, I thought I would just come on by."

She let out a loud sigh. "Get to the point."

"Hubby is the point. You want Buddy to stay happy. I want Buddy to stay happy." He walked over and poured himself a drink. "I also want five thousand dollars, sister dear."

"Listen to me, you piece of slime! No more damned money!" she shouted.

"Ooh, such a temper tantrum. It's only money. I'm sure your marriage is worth it."

"You heard what I said. Not one penny more."

"What if I told you this will be the end of it?"

"Man, have I heard that before." Marcia took a sip of her drink.

"It's true this time. Things are finally starting to come together for 'ole Philip."

"Whose feet are you holding to the fire this time?"

His thin lips twisted into a smirk. "In the old days, you would have said something much earthier. You were much more fun back then. You've become a bore." His cold eyes slid over her body. "You used to do anything to anybody for the right price. I guess old Buddy is getting all of your action now."

Philip poured himself another shot. "Still haven't told old Buddy all your secrets, have you?" He laughed. "Of course you haven't."

"You never fail to go for the jugular. Just like any other predator."

Philip smiled. "Broads like you are such easy prey."

"You know, one of these days, someone is going to kill you. When they do, I hope to hell I'm around to see it."

"It will take somebody a lot tougher than you. I'll be back on Monday. Have the money."

He sauntered out the door, leaving her to glare at his back.

5

Nancy Osborne's Treasure Trove was one of the original shops on Lower Greenville Avenue. It became immensely successful because of her unique talent of recognizing things of beauty that were hidden in one way or another. She had begun by hitting every garage and estate sale in the State, buying wisely, and restoring the finds she found with true artistry.

Now she was somebody. Her renovated house was near completion, and her collection of antiques was the envy of her competitors. She had everything she wanted--everything except Philip Barnes.

. . . . .

Dinner at Hoffbrau had indeed paid off. Nancy lay deliciously exhausted. She watched Philip with lust and possession as he walked naked into the kitchen. He was indeed an animal, she thought, in every way.

Yet, no matter how many times they made love, Nancy always felt as if she were alone. Technically, he was an incredible lover, but she just could not reach him. It was one reason she so desperately wanted him. She yearned to see an expression of love in his eyes and feel it in his touch. He had never once kissed her. Philip had told her at the beginning that he did not kiss on the lips.

Nancy had heard he was also seeing Taylor Niedringhaus. Ironically, they had met through her. Taylor had come into her shop, bought a gorgeous love seat, and Nancy made the mistake of asking Philip to deliver it.

It never occurred to her that Taylor of the megabucks would look twice at Philip. She should have known that people, like antiques, are not always what they seem on the outside.

Nancy felt a chill through her body as she suddenly had a mental picture of Philip and Taylor together. Then the real fear came. What if Philip left her? She lit another joint and dragged deeply, holding in the smoke as long as she could.

Philip came back with wine for Nancy and a beer for himself. He stretched out on the bed beside her, took a long hit from the joint, then passed it back to her.

Had she not been stoned, Nancy would never have confronted him. She could not seem to stop herself. "Someone saw you having lunch with Taylor Niedringhaus the other day."

"Yeah, we had lunch. So what?"

"Bet she's not as good in bed as I am."

"I told you before, what I do is none of your business."

She ran her fingers across his stomach. "No one else knows everything about you like I do."

Philip abruptly sat up on one elbow, pushing her hand away. "Just what do you think you know?"

"Well, let me see. I know about the trouble with the Henderson woman, and about the little side business you and Hunter have going from time to time."

He grabbed her arm. She knew from his expression she had gone too far. She wasn't afraid, though Philip was not a man to mess with.

"I would be very careful about what I said if I were you. Understand?"

"Darling, of course I understand. I don't care what you've done. There will be no one else for me. Just you—always."

Philip relaxed his hold on her arm. "Always is a long time."

"We fit together like two pieces of a puzzle. I will never let you go."

He smiled. "Sounds like a threat. The second one I've had today."

She leaned over and nibbled on his earlobe. "It's not a threat, babe," she whispered. "It's a promise."

6

The major airlines had moved from Love Field in favor of DFW Airport, leaving only tiny Southwest Airlines to fill the gap. The area had become rundown almost in a matter of minutes.

Jim Hunter hated the Mexicans and African-Americans who moved in, or the spics and spooks as he referred to them, together with what he considered white trash. He knew his family was safe. No one liked to mess with a cop—especially Jim Hunter—who had a reputation as a guy who would shoot first and ask questions later.

Hunter entered his house through the garage and stopped at the refrigerator for a beer. He called out and when no one answered, continued down the hallway to the bathroom.

"Hey, Cathy, you in there?" His tone was surprisingly soft.

"Yes, daddy. I'm taking a bath."

"Okay if I come in?"

"Uh, uh." She giggled as the bubbles tickled her nose. Her long blond hair dripped with soapsuds. The ten-year-old body had not yet erupted into adolescence. Soon she would give up playing with the toy boat floating in the water in favor of clothes and boys. For now, her blue eyes held the beautiful, wondrous innocence of childhood.

"How about I wash your back like I used to when you were little?"

"Mama says I am too old for you to wash my back."

Ethel Hunter came silently down the hall and stood behind her husband. She wore a waitress uniform. Her lank dishwater-blond hair surrounded a face that looked as if she had been tired for a long time. Her rounded shoulders added to her air of defeat.

"What do you think you are doing?" she snapped.

Hunter didn't bother to look up. "I am talking to Cathy, as you can plainly see."

"Come on into the kitchen for a minute. I want to talk to you."

She turned and walked rapidly down the hallway. Hunter reluctantly followed her. She closed the door and turned to face him, her face livid.

"She's not your daughter. Stay away from her when she don't have her clothes on. I've seen the way you look at her." Ethel Hunter had good reason to be afraid of her husband. Now her anger overrode her fear.

Hunter's lip curled. "Or what?"

"I'll kill you if you ever touch her."

He shoved her against the counter as he went to the refrigerator for another beer. "You ain't gonna do nothin, you dried up old hag."

Her eyes narrowed. "You'd do well to remember what I told you."

· · · · ·

Ethel finished the last of the dinner dishes and wished for the hundredth time that Jim would let her buy a dishwasher. She had spent years wishing for things he promised and never delivered.

Evenings were her favorite time when he worked the three-to- eleven shift and she and Cathy could have the evenings to themselves. Unfortunately, he would start the eleven-to-seven shift on Monday. As usual, he was stretched out on the couch, watching TV.

She was aware he had been getting some strange calls. "You in some kind of trouble again?" she asked.

His eyes did not move from the screen. "Nah. Just some broad I gave a ticket tried to get me and Barnes in trouble. She was out messin' around and got beat up."

"What did you do?"

"I told you, we didn't do nothin'."

"I'll bet. We both know what you are."

"You know, one of these days I may decide to dump you. I would get custody of Cathy, too. I'd fix it so you're found with a little nose candy and get sent up for a while. How would you like that?"

"You won't do much dumping if you're dead."

Hunter reached for his cap and started for the door.

"Where are you going now?"

"Away from you, old bitch."

"Just remember, leave me and mine alone."

• • • • •

Ethel glanced at the clock, put her book away, and turned off the bedroom light.

The bars were now closed. Jim would soon come stumbling home. She huddled in the old recliner, moving her hand over the gun in the pocket of her robe. She'd made Cathy lock her bedroom door. It was just a precaution, she told herself.

She heard a noise and got up from the chair. She did not turn on the light. She went to the door and opened it a crack. Jim stood outside Cathy's door. Ethel held her breath as he turned the knob several times, then frowned as he turned away and staggered toward their bedroom.

Ethel hurried across the room, crawled into her bed, and pretended to be asleep.

Jim muttered to himself as he undressed and crawled into the other twin bed.

Ethel waited until the sound of his rhythmic snoring filled the room. She quickly undressed, laid her robe on a chair, and slid the gun under her pillow.

Jim had given her the .38 police special for her and Cathy's protection—and their protection was exactly what she intended to use it for.

7

"Clarice, it's Emily. I'm sorry to call you so early."

"What's the matter?"

"I don't have any clothes. How can I go home with no clothes?"

"Damn. I completely forgot."

"I also have to be dressed when I talk with Lt. Bannister."

"Walmart is open. How about sizes?"

"Just some sweats, size small. Maybe some flip-flops, size six."

"I can't believe how tiny you are. Consider it handled. See you soon."

Emily struggled to get her hair into a ponytail. Reaching her arms behind her head caused considerable pain in her ribs. She finally succeeded. A stranger with raccoon eyes and a bulbous nose stared back at her from the mirror. She wondered how long it would be before the swelling went down. She was told the pain in her ribs would be with her for a while. Better not to wonder when her mind would heal.

Maybe Dan would feel differently today after he had a chance to think things through. Emily sighed. Time to stop wishful thinking and face reality. Right now, she had too many realities to face.

Clarice arrived with an armload of packages. A huge stuffed coyote with a long tail and fluffy ears hung over her shoulder. "Could not resist him," she said with a grin as she handed him over.

Emily clutched the stuffed animal to her. "He's adorable. I love him."

It was the first time Clarice had seen Emily smile. "Do you need me to help you get dressed?"

"No. I think I can do it."

"I'll step outside. Yell if you need me."

Emily dressed hurriedly and called Clarice to come in. Mr. coyote rested on her lap.

Clarice smiled. "You look so much better."

"You know, I've been wondering about your Center," Emily said. "Tell me more about it."

"I started it a few years ago." Clarice looked down at her hands. "Shortly after my daughter Laurie was murdered."

"I'm so sorry."

"It's okay." Clarice's eyes misted over. "Laurie was a nurse here. She was murdered on her way home one night. Her killer hasn't been found—yet. I will never give up hope." She smiled.

"The Center helps women in trouble, from a place to stay to professional therapy for women like yourself—women who must rebuild their lives."

"A place of hope. It must give you a wonderful feeling to know you are needed," Emily said.

"The Center is the only thing that gets me up in the morning. Enough about me. What are we going to do about you?"

Emily frowned. "What do you mean?"

"You need to heal your emotional scars as well as the physical ones. I know Dr. Asher explained to you about post-traumatic stress disorder. Sometimes the real trauma takes a while to set in. The Center has psychiatrists who specialize in post-traumatic stress disorder. It's critical for you to work with one."

"I'll be fine as soon as they put Hunter and Barnes away where they belong."

"What if that doesn't happen?"

Emily was a long time answering. "Then I'll have no choice but to kill them."

"Don't worry, Emily. Lt. Bannister will get to the bottom of things." Clarice looked up as Bannister tapped on the door and walked in. "Speak of the devil."

"Morning ladies." He turned to Emily. "Mrs. Henderson, I'm Lt. Bannister. I would like to get your statement for the record. I'll also bring you up to date on what we've learned so far."

Emily withdrew into herself. "Okay."

"Why don't you just start with the dinner Friday night," he said.

Emily took a deep breath. She'd forgotten about her broken ribs. She exhaled slowly and forced herself not to cry out from the pain. Bannister would think she was looking for sympathy. One thing was certain—the new pain pills had not kicked in. "I went to my company's annual party at the West-End Steakhouse," she began.

"What time did you leave there?"

"About eight-thirty."

"Were you alone?"

"Of course I was alone. I was driving north on Harry Hines. Just past Walnut Hill, I noticed a brown car behind me. Its siren was on and the red light atop the car was flashing. I pulled over into the parking lot of Casa Miguel. I thought they just wanted to pass. I was wrong. They were after me." Emily's voice caught.

Bannister nodded. "Just take your time, Mrs. Henderson. I know this is difficult for you."

The pills must have kicked in because Emily discovered there was less pain when she breathed. Her voice was steadier when she continued.

"The older one—Hunter—said I had an outstanding warrant. They put me in the front seat of their car for the drive downtown. When I questioned why we had passed Industrial Boulevard and were on the freeway, the younger one—Barnes—put his gun against the side of my cheek."

Emily managed to block her emotions as she described the beatings and her escape. She told of waking in the morning and making her way to the main road where the Fitzsimmons found her.

Bannister took some papers from his briefcase. "Mrs. Henderson, I questioned Hunter and Barnes at length yesterday evening. They were on the three-to-eleven shift Friday night. They were driving a brown car, like you said, because they were cracking down on drunk drivers along the Harry Hines strip. They said you had probably read about it in the papers.

"They insisted they never laid eyes on you Friday night. They mentioned an altercation they had with you a couple of weeks ago."

Emily began rubbing her arms as she rocked back and forth in her chair. "What in the world are you talking about? Can't you see they're lying?"

"The problem is so far we've only seen where you said you were. My men combed the area where you were found. Unfortunately, it's been raining non-stop, and they didn't find much. There were still signs where you were on the river bank—the broken branches that stopped your fall. They found marks in the mud where you dragged yourself onto the main road. Otherwise, there was nothing."

Emily could only stare at him.

"What concerns me, Mrs. Henderson, is when I checked the computer, I found a citation was issued to you two weeks ago for running a stop sign—just like Hunter said."

Emily's mouth dropped open. "That is impossible."

"Is your driver's license 07892986?"

Emily sighed as she shook her head. "I don't know. Sounds right."

He handed her a copy of the ticket. "Someone only initialed the ticket. It made me suspicious. I questioned Officer Hunter since he issued it. He claims they pulled you over and an argument ensued. You were adamant that you had not run the stop sign. You refused to sign the ticket."

Emily just kept shaking her head.

"Hunter isn't much of a people person. He said Officer Barnes handled the situation, told you it would be acceptable for you to just initial the ticket to show you'd received it. Hunter said you were very upset about the possibility of your husband finding out."

"Surely you can't believe them!" Emily cried.

"I'm only telling you what they contend," Bannister replied. "Hunter and Barnes insist you named them as the men who kidnapped you in retaliation for giving you the ticket."

"Lieutenant, that's nothing but lies! I am telling you, I never laid eyes on them before Friday night. They certainly never gave me any ticket!"

"Mrs. Henderson, I wanted to let you know what has turned up so far. Our investigation is just beginning. We will be checking out Casa Miguel. If you're telling the truth, someone may remember seeing you in the parking lot. The flashing light on the brown car might have been noticed. A lot of follow-up needs to be done."

"IF I'm telling the truth!" Emily cried.

She sighed as she fought for control. "Dan will be here soon. Would you tell him everything you've learned? I just can't deal with anything more."

"Okay. I'll take care of it." Bannister nodded and left the room.

Emily turned to Clarice. "Do you believe me?"

"Yes," Clarice replied without hesitation.

"I think you're the only one who does. I need to be alone to try to get my head together before I have to face Dan. I want you to know I appreciate everything you're doing for me, Clarice."

• • • • •

Clarice caught Bannister's arm as she came out of Emily's room. "Wait a minute. I want to talk to you."

"Clarice, I'm a cop. Before you say anything, I want you to know that I, and every cop in this city, will take it hard if Hunter and Barnes are guilty of this. Particularly patrol cops. Those guys put their lives on the line every day. Two rotten apples out of over thirty thousand of us are two too many."

"I understand how you feel, Lou. But damn it, did you have to tell her about the ticket now?"

"She needs to know everything I know when I know it. I make it a practice to never discount my gut feelings about people. Everything points to Emily Henderson lying through her teeth. Still, I would bet my pension she's telling the truth. Now, all we have to do is prove it."

Clarice nodded. "She would have to be delusional to name Hunter and Barnes instead of who really assaulted her. She is not delusional. Sorry I snapped at you. I get a little carried away sometimes."

Bannister grinned as he chucked her under the chin. "Someday soon I plan to carry you away—into the sunset, my sweet."

8

Emily searched Dan's face as he came into her room. His expression gave no clue of his reaction to his talk with Lt. Bannister. He was busy complaining about all the paperwork he had to fill out for her release.

Her eyes remained wary as Dan kissed her lightly on her unbandaged cheek. It took all of her self-control not to turn her head away.

"So, Emily, ready to go?"

"I guess so." The only thing to be packed was the plastic hospital sack containing her medications. "Dr. Asher called in some new prescriptions. Can we pick them up on our way home?" She wondered when he intended to bring up the kidnapping.

Dan made a face as he spotted Mr. Coyote. "Aren't you a little old for stuffed animals?"

Emily's face flushed, but she refused to answer.

Nurse Walker arrived and settled Emily in a wheelchair. "Hospital rules. You cannot leave under your own power, young lady."

As they made their way to the front entrance, Nurse Walker turned to Dan. "You might want to drive around here and park. I'll help settle Emily into the car."

Dan drove to the hospital entrance and waited as Nurse Walker helped Emily into the car, making sure she was comfortable and her seatbelt fastened. Emily clutched Mr. Coyote as they moved into traffic. The minutes went by silently until the tension became unbearable. Finally, she broke the silence. "Did you and Lt. Bannister discuss the investigation?"

"Yes," he replied. "Lt. Bannister seems competent enough to solve the case." His face was turned away, so she couldn't see his expression.

"I'll call your office in the morning and say you were in an accident. You can stay home until next week. Your face should look better by then," he said.

Oh, yes, she thought, you wouldn't like it if anyone asked about what happened to me.

"You don't give a damn about me, do you?" she blurted out.

He didn't answer.

Her body sagged against the door, and she fought the impulse to jump from the car. They rode home in silence.

• • • • •

Emily woke with a start. The medication had worn off, and the pain was unbearable. She reached for the Tylenol Three and a glass of water from the nightstand, then burrowed back under the bedspread, three blankets, and her old chenille robe which was buttoned up to her neck. She curled into a fetal position, waiting for the pain to subside.

Eventually she drifted into a fitful sleep, dreaming she stood before one of the two floor-to-ceiling windows in her living room. Young men mingled around her porch, their faces obscured by masks. She was certain they planned to harm her. They called to her as they came toward her window. It was impossible to understand their words.

In her dream, Emily hurried to the window. She found the slide bolt and tried to lock it, but a hand was already inside the window, struggling to keep it open.

She frantically hit at the hand. As they withdrew it, she slid the bolt into place, then watched, horrified, as the masked men moved toward the other window.

She stumbled and fell in her frenzy to get to the window and lock it before they reached it. Finally, both windows were secured, and she fell back on the couch, panting from exhaustion.

She looked up and whimpered. Two of the masked men had somehow gotten inside. One of them ordered her to sit perfectly still. They tore off their masks. Hunter and Barnes leered at her. Emily hid her face with her arms, but nothing happened. She finally found the courage to face them, but they had miraculously disappeared.

Still half asleep, she told herself it was a nightmare, yet it was impossible for her to wake up. As the nightmare continued, she lay in bed with the covers pulled up around her neck.

The house was silent. Then came the sound of the outside door opening.

She waited in the darkness, afraid even to breathe, yet no one appeared. Then she heard another noise. Someone was moving toward the bedroom. Cowering in the bed, she tried to call out for help, but couldn't. She sat bolt upright as the door opened, straining to scream—and woke up.

Her bed was in shambles. The covers had fallen to the floor, and Emily was drenched with sweat, relieved and exhausted. She recoiled as she caught a glimpse of herself in the mirror. Her matted hair, swollen face, and wild bloodshot eyes stared back. She reached for Dan's cigarettes, but her hand shook so badly the package fell to the floor.

She forced herself to get out of bed and tiptoe to the den—Dan's trophy room. The walls were filled with poor dead animals and fish—his prizes. She was surprised he had not stuffed a dove. She smiled at her caustic thought. Dan was asleep on the couch with the TV drowning out the sound of his snoring.

With a sigh, she returned to the bedroom. She fingered Clarice's card in the pocket of her robe as she looked at the clock. Clarice had said to call day or night, but did that mean calling at two a.m.?

"Clarice, it's Emily. I'm sorry to wake you."

"I was reading and just drifted off. Hold on a minute." Clarice put the recliner in an upright position. "Okay, I'm awake. What's wrong?"

"Oh, Clarice, I had a horrible nightmare. I'm afraid to go back to sleep."

"Where's Dan? Isn't he there with you?"

"Asleep in the den. He—wait." Emily listened, then continued in a whisper. "I have to go. The TV just went off. Dan must be awake. Can I come to the Center tomorrow?"

"Of course. Do you know how to get there?"

Emily glanced at the card, then slipped it into the pocket of her robe. "I'll find it."

She replaced the receiver and switched off the lamp. A few minutes later, the bedroom door opened. The den's light behind him silhouetted Dan in the doorway. For one incredulous moment, she was afraid he planned to get into bed with her, but he simply took a blanket and pillows from the closet and left the room. She heard his retreating steps down the hallway, then the TV came back on. With trembling hands, she finally managed to light a cigarette and sat in the dark, waiting for morning.

• • • • • •

Emily had no idea how long she had been sitting at the kitchen table. Her full cup of coffee was cold. She tensed as Dan walked in. His expression betrayed annoyance at her appearance.

She was sure she looked a mess this morning with her uncombed hair, bruised face and bloody bandage, which probably needed changing. She clutched her robe higher around her neck. Dan leaned over her, hesitated, then gave her a peck on the cheek.

"Be careful, Dan. You don't want to catch anything."

"Did you sleep okay?" he asked, ignoring her remark.

He was dressed in a suit and tie, ready for work. He poured a cup of coffee and stood at the counter. Emily stared at her hands.

"I asked if you slept okay. I passed out on the couch." He sipped his coffee. "Look, I have a lot going on today. Do you want someone from church to stay with you?"

"No."

Dan put his cup in the sink and reached for his attaché case. "Suit yourself."

"Nothing will ever be the same between us, will it?"

Ignoring her, Dan walked toward the garage door.

"Damn it, turn around and look at me."

He stood in the doorway. "I'm afraid looking at you is not very pleasant. Why don't you take a shower—clean yourself up?"

Emily's head jerked back as if he had slapped her.

The garage door opened and closed. He was gone. She felt only relief.

9

Emily dug her fingernails into the soap to remove the imaginary dirt. No matter how long she washed, she didn't feel clean. She averted her gaze from the mirror, unable to look at her bruised body. She changed the bandage on her face. No point trying to cover the bruises on her face with makeup.

At least the swelling had gone down a little.

She started to cry. Damn it, she scolded herself, crying won't help. Anger is better. She would make sure those two bastards got what they deserved. Maybe then she could look at herself in the mirror.

Emily started out of the house, remembered her pills, and hurried back.

She stopped to take another. Thank God for drugs. There was no way she could deal with the pain and everything else without them.

She drove down Turtle Creek, then turned right onto Fairmount. She drove slowly, looking for 4316. She circled the block. This time, she spotted a small wrought-iron signpost. The plate said 4316 Fairmount, Women's Crisis Center.

Emily parked the car and got out. A flight of steps led to a landing where she stopped awhile to rest, then began to climb the second flight of steps.

The steep hill on either side was lush with newly mowed grass. Her guess was that an old house was torn down, and another built further back on the lot, out of view. She sat down to catch her breath several more times before reaching the top.

Emily had not expected anything like this. The house sat in the middle of a double lot. It sported a fresh coat of white paint with teal blue shutters.

Blooming crepe myrtles, some with pink blossoms, others with white, filled the yard, along with azaleas and a myriad of vegetable beds. Rocking chairs were scattered around the wide porch which surrounded the house. An empty porch swing beckoned in the breeze.

She saw Clarice cutting roses from one of the many bushes which nestled next to the house.

"What a beautiful place!" Emily exclaimed. "I expected something..."

Clarice interrupted her, smiling. "Like a hospital?"

"Yes. I guess I was."

Emily followed her inside. Hardwood floors in the living and dining rooms gleamed with a rich patina. She admired several well-worn, still beautiful oriental rugs. The furniture was a mish-mash of styles, but it all looked clean and comfortable.

"We buy everything from the Salvation Army," Clarice told her. "We help them—they help us."

The yeasty aroma of baking bread came from a gigantic kitchen. Clarice opened a cloth-covered basket. "The rolls are still warm."

Emily bit into one. "Um, wonderful." She helped herself to another.

Clarice poured them each a steaming cup of coffee and placed everything on a tray. "Let me show you our sunroom."

Emily followed her down a hall, glancing into several of the rooms as they went. Everything was sparse and serviceable, yet homey.

French doors led into the sunroom. Two walls of the room were waist-to-ceiling windows overlooking the yard, shadowed by a pecan tree. The furniture here was all white wicker—couch, settee, two rocking chairs, and a coffee table. Plants were everywhere and needlepoint pictures hung from the two remaining walls.

Emily settled into one of the rocking chairs. "This room makes me feel like nothing bad could ever happen here."

Clarice nodded. "It always lifts my spirits to sit in here. We have tried to make the entire Center a place where women can believe life will get better. A place which gives us all hope." She closed the French doors behind them. "Now, tell me what's going on with you, young lady?"

Emily rocked in her chair. "I'm handling the physical pain—or kind of handling it—thanks to the drugs. Mentally, I'm not doing so well."

"I can't deal with the injustice of it all, including Dan's reaction. We have been married for eighteen months and I suddenly feel I don't know him. Or maybe I just didn't want to see him as he really is. Now I find him repulsive and can't bear the thought of him touching me ever again. My life with him is over."

"Remember, this has also been quite a shock for Dan. Things may not be as hopeless as you feel right now."

Emily choked back a sob. "Why do I feel so guilty? I did nothing wrong. Oh, Clarice, I am beginning to question my sanity."

"There is not a woman who has walked through these doors who didn't feel guilty. They all ask the same question—'Why me?'"

Emily nodded. "I have asked myself the same question over and over."

Clarice shook her head. "I don't have any answers for you or myself. I ask myself over and over, 'why Laurie'?"

"Oh. I forgot about your daughter."

"The rage will never go away until I find out who killed her, and why."

Emily sighed. "One minute I feel anger. The next minute I feel terrible depression. I am certain of one thing. I will not stop until Hunter and Barnes' lives are destroyed, as they have destroyed mine."

Clarice spoke softly. "I understand very well what you are feeling."

Emily stared out the window. "I have to get away from Dan. I've decided to check into a motel."

"Emily, I don't think that's such a good idea. Come here to the Center. Dr. Asher has made you an appointment with Dr. DeMarco for three o'clock tomorrow afternoon."

Emily continued as if she hadn't heard. "Dreams and reality all run together." She turned back to the window and watched the children who were playing below.

"When I'm awake, I try to make sense of what's happened. I'm afraid to sleep because the demons are waiting." She covered her face with her hands and sobbed.

"Please stay, Emily," Clarice pleaded. "You'll be safe here at the Center."

Emily shook her head. "Not yet. Something keeps nagging at me. It's just beyond the edge of my mind. I have to be alone to find out what it is, away from everyone."

"I have a house on Grapevine Lake," Clarice told her. "If you insist on being alone, you could go there. Then you wouldn't be isolated. The lake is ringed with houses and shops. It's a wine-making center and also has great antique shops. I would feel much better if you stayed there rather than at a motel."

Emily's face brightened. "It sounds perfect. Please let me stay there—just for tonight. I give you my word. I will come back tomorrow and see Dr. DeMarco."

"Will you let Dan know where you're going?"

"I doubt he'd care, but I'll leave a note." It just won't say Clarice's lake house, she thought to herself.

"If you are positive this is what you want, I won't try to talk you out of it. God knows everyone has their own way of dealing with things. I will worry about you. There is a phone, and I want you to call me as soon as you arrive."

"I will. You're the best, Clarice. I can't wait to get started."

Clarice laughed. "Can you hold on long enough for me to write out directions?"

．　．　．　．　．

Emily had packed and started out the door when she remembered the note.

She hurriedly scribbled one and set it on the coffee table in the den. She started to leave, then stopped and moved to the gun case which housed Dan's rifles, shotguns, and handguns. She found the .38 pistol which Dan had insisted she learn to shoot. He kept bullets in the drawer below. She found the right caliber, stuffed the gun and bullets into her purse, and hurried through the kitchen into the garage.

She shuddered as she stared at her convertible. It was Dan's until he drove it into the ground. He dumped it on her after trading her car in on the Honda.

Dan had driven the pickup to work, so she would take the new Honda. He never allowed her to drive it. He would be furious. She didn't care.

She pulled onto the street just as a storm erupted. Rain came down in torrents. Clarice had said her house wasn't far, that it sat right on the lake. But she was suddenly frightened. She told herself to snap out of it. Stop it, Emily, you have faced death and survived. You are strong. Just give yourself time to heal. For heaven's sake, you've only been out of the hospital for one day.

Clarice was right. It didn't take long to get to the lake, and Emily easily found the driveway to Clarice's lake house. She parked in front, grabbed her night case and Mr. Coyote, and hurried to the porch. The key was in the mailbox where Clarice had said it would be.

Inside, drenched but safe, she bolted the door behind her. The cabin smelled pleasantly of ashes and burned logs. Walking across the room, she opened the patio window drapes and looked out. The lake and storm were one—a wild swirl of water and clouds, beautiful and majestic. She lit the logs which were already laid in the fireplace.

She found a robe, took off her wet clothes, and changed into it. She was warm, but the pain pill had worn off and her entire body hurt. Half a bottle of brandy sat on the kitchen counter. She found a glass and poured herself a drink, then called the Center as she'd promised. Clarice was out. Theona promised to give her the message.

The glow from the fire was the only light in the living room. The flames danced, making pictures on the wall. Emily stretched out on the couch and took a pill, washing it down with the brandy, which burned her tongue deliciously. She began to feel relaxed and warm. Clutching Mr. Coyote, she closed her eyes and fell asleep.

Sometime later the cold woke her. It had grown dark outside and the fire inside had burned down to glowing ash. Then, as if a movie had started inside her head, she began reliving scenes of that horrible night.

Her body trembled as sudden realization washed over her. Emily had believed they chose her at random, but she had been wrong. She now remembered Barnes' words, "Let's just get the job done and get back to town." The job? Their job was to kill her! My God! But why?

Emily removed the gun from her purse, carefully loaded the bullets into the chambers of the cylinder, and held it on her lap. She swallowed another pill with a slug of biting, warming brandy. She stared into the embers as if the answers to all her questions were hidden there.

IO

At Precinct 523, the night shift was beginning. It had been storming for the past three hours, which meant a rash of traffic accidents and a long night. Hunter was in a good mood, even though they were on the graveyard shift.

Barnes followed him out of the station through the driving rain and into their squad car.

Hunter shook the water off his hat and threw it on the floor in the back. "See, I told you everything would work out." His florid face broke into a smile.

"Just drop it," Barnes snapped.

"I'm used to handling stuff like this." Hunter continued. "We're in the clear. You can take my word for it. The traffic ticket was a nice touch, don't you think? It never hurts to cover your ass because you gotta plan for somethin' to go wrong."

Barnes smirked. "We both know you're not smart enough to have thought of the ticket. I've got a feeling the bitch isn't gonna let it drop. We're not out of trouble yet." He lit a cigarette and blew the smoke at Hunter, knowing it would annoy him. "You said she was dead. How the hell could you miss her at such close range?"

"Hey, I shot her in the head. I thought she was a goner. Besides, it wasn't my damned fault that car came along," Hunter replied angrily.

"You did get rid of the throw-away?" Barnes' voice dripped sarcasm.

"Yeah. You're right. Let's just shut up about it."

Barnes propped his knees against the dashboard. "Wake me when it's time for coffee."

· · · · ·

It would be dawn soon. The rain had stopped and thick fog had rolled in over the city. The patrol car waited at a red light at Harry Hines and Royal. Hunter drummed his fingers on the steering wheel, eager for the light to change. There was no traffic at this time of the morning and it was almost time to go home. They crossed the intersection and turned down Morgan Street for a last pass-by of the deserted warehouse district. A stalled car faced them, its hood up, and the emergency lights blinking.

Hunter peered through the fog. "Looks like a motorist in distress."

"If it's a woman, I'll do the talking. You just do the mechanics," Barnes snapped.

"Sure, kid. Sure."

They parked across the street from the stalled car. A lone woman sat behind the wheel, her face obscured by a slouch hat.

"The broad is probably out of gas," Hunter said.

Both men got out of the squad car. Hunter walked to the front of the stalled car while Barnes stopped at the driver's window.

"Got a problem, ma'am?" Barnes asked.

The woman nodded. The hat kept her face obscured.

"Step out of the car and I'll give it a try."

Barnes opened the door, and the woman got out. She kept her head down—her face still averted.

She turned to face Barnes as he held the door. Her gloved hand was already out of the pocket of her trench coat—the .38 pointed at his chest. Too late, Barnes started to react. Two cracks broke the silence, and he fell to the pavement.

The woman stepped around him. Hunter started back from the front of the car as he reached for his gun. His eyes darted to Barnes lying in the street.

The woman spoke calmly. "Don't."

His hand froze in mid-air, and his eyes widened in disbelief.

"You!"

The woman smiled as she aimed for his stomach and fired at point-blank range.

As Hunter fell, she fired a second shot. He lay face-up on the pavement—not moving. She stood over him, carefully aimed the gun at his groin, and fired again. She walked back to Barnes, who lay on his side. She rolled him over until he was lying face-up on the pavement. She aimed the gun at his groin and fired, then stepped around their bodies and closed the hood. There was the sound of the engine starting, then the car disappeared into the fog.

• • • • •

Bannister parked in front of the four patrol cars that formed a barricade and whose headlights illuminated the scene of the crime. The medical examiner walked away from the scene, finished for now. Ambulance lights whirred while the paramedics prepared to move the bodies to the morgue. Hunter and Barnes were already in body bags.

"It was a woman, Lieutenant. Mr. Jamison, our witness, said she was wearing a hat and high-heeled shoes. He had heard what he thought was a car backfiring and came out to look. He made out two bodies in the street, and the woman getting into a car. He said the fog was too thick to see her license plate or the model of her car."

Bannister unzipped one of the body bags. His face tightened as he stared down at Hunter's body. He slowly closed it and walked to the other bag. He looked weary as he moved to a patrol car and picked up the mike.

"Ed, this is Bannister. Get out an all-points on Emily Henderson. Yeah, for questioning in the Hunter and Barnes homicides. Call me when you have her in custody."

. . . . .

It was nine o'clock when Emily turned into her driveway. Dan was sure to have left for work by now. As she started up the walk, two men emerged from a parked car and blocked her path.

"Emily Henderson?" asked the one who had his gun drawn.

"Yes."

"I am Detective Addington, Homicide." He nodded toward the other man. "That is Detective Young."

Her eyes grew wide. "Yes," she whispered finally.

"You are wanted downtown, Mrs. Henderson."

"What for?"

"For questioning in the murders of Officers James Hunter and Philip Barnes. You may remain silent."

"No. It's another trick." Emily tried to push past them. She must get to her car and to the Center where she would be safe.

Addington caught her arm. "Put your hands behind your back."

She looked up at him. What had he said about Hunter and Barnes? Something about murder.

"What did you say before, officer?"

"I said you are wanted for questioning in the murders of Officers James Hunter and Philip Barnes."

"You mean they're dead? Hunter and Barnes are dead?" She began to laugh hysterically as Addington placed the cuffs on her for the ride downtown.

II

Emily hesitated outside the jail's visiting room. She felt anger and fear at the same time. What if she became hysterical again?

What would Dan say? The last thing in the world she wanted was to face him now.

Dan didn't bother to get up when she walked into the room, which didn't much surprise her. She smoothed down the ugly prison garb, hating the feel of it. She felt trapped and claustrophobic as she faced her husband across the table.

His eyes slid past her face.

"Did you know you are being charged with capital murder?"

She winced at the sound of his voice. It was as harsh as the policeman's when he interrogated her.

Emily started to answer, but found she was unable to speak. She was mute. Her eyes darted around the room for some kind of sanctuary. There was none. She slumped in her chair, stared down at the table, and tried to remember how long she had been in jail. It seemed like several days. She wanted to ask Dan why it had taken him so long to come and get her.

"You will need an attorney other than the court-appointed one you had for the arraignment," he said impatiently.

Emily nodded, not lifting her head.

"My God, Emily, capital murder! Are you really crazy?"

She raised her head. She could only stare back at him. You think I am capable of murder, she thought. How could he believe that?

Please get me out of here. No, she thought, you are not taking me home. Emily rubbed her forearms as she rocked back and forth in her chair. This seemed to irritate Dan, so she kept doing it.

"They charged you with killing two policemen, Emily. Don't you understand?"

Something in her snapped, and she was no longer a cowering, frightened woman. Anger raged through her body. Her eyes blazed as she glared back at him.

Yes, I understand, she thought. All you do is accuse me. I am not a whore. I told the truth about Hunter and Barnes kidnaping me.

"If you had stayed home where you belonged, none of this would have happened," Dan said.

There it was. Everything had happened because she had disobeyed him and went to the dinner. Emily took a deep breath and let it out slowly. The pain from her broken ribs felt good. She realized Dan was convinced she had murdered Hunter and Barnes.

"If they did what you claim, I probably wouldn't blame you," he continued, not looking at her.

She ignored his comment and remained mute.

Finally, he returned her gaze, then his eyes slid off her face.

Her rage dissipated and was replaced by a great sadness. Yes, she thought, you believe I killed them. I can see it in your eyes. She smiled to herself. She realized he was afraid of her.

"You just leave everything to me," he told her. "I'll get you a lawyer and we'll plead insanity."

Emily laughed—a short, bitter laugh. She was surprised she could finally speak. "Aren't you afraid to be around an insane person? You wouldn't let me pursue pressing charges. Now you're going to say I'm insane. I don't want your help, Dan. I'll take care of myself."

"Yeah," he smirked, "you've done such a fine job so far."

She scraped back her chair and stood up. "I will be fighting for my life, Dan. I refuse to have to look into your eyes and see what you think is my guilt reflected there. Stay away from me."

"You really are crazy! Do you think your precious friend, Clarice, will come up with a lawyer? Well, she can just come up with the money, too."

Emily was perfectly calm now. She leaned over until she was in his face. "Pay attention, Dan. I want you to leave now and never come back. I never want to see or hear from you again. Do you understand?"

The stunned look on his face made her smile. He grabbed her arm. She waited, staring at his hand, until he finally released it. She turned away from him without another word and pushed the button for the matron.

PART TWO

12

A vintage Cadillac convertible inched its way along the alley. Coulter McBride had bought it, fully restored, with the proceeds of his first big win. He still remembered the case and sometimes wondered what ever happened to Tony Scarlito, the man he had gotten off. The car was in cherry condition. He maintained it himself and never let a parking lot attendant touch it.

He also never drove the car when he was drinking, which explained why the long, Levi-encased legs of his good friend, Johnny Thompson, were currently folded under the steering wheel.

Coulter still wore his work uniform—navy suit, white shirt, and conservative navy and burgundy striped tie. The top button of the shirt was now undone, and the tie loosened. His straight jet-black hair and high cheekbones spoke of his Cherokee heritage, while the cornflower-blue eyes spoke of his Irish ancestors.

He sipped steadily on a bourbon and water. "You gotta know when to quit," Coulter opined to himself. "Soc needs to quit fighting and I need to quit the law." He sighed and took another drink. "God, Johnny, he's been gone two days."

"I don't know how the hell you talked me into this, counselor. You're drunker'n seven hundred dollars."

Coulter nodded. "Yeah, I know. We can't give up, though. This is Soc we're talking about."

Johnny sighed. "Coulter, we ain't never gonna find your damned cat."

"Mary told me where to look. He'll be here."

"Well, that's different. If Mary says he's here, then he's here."

Coulter peered into the alley. "Hold on a minute." He retrieved a flashlight from the glove compartment and grabbed the blanket Mary had given him. He turned on the flash and started down the alley.

He was just over six feet tall, thin, and wiry. Opponents from various drinking establishments made the mistake of thinking thin was weak. They didn't know he had once been a Golden Gloves champion.

Coulter's face was marred by a single scar in the shape of a V in the middle of his forehead. He'd received it at the age of six when Maureen Maguire beaned him and split the skin wide open when he tried to kiss her.

"Soc? Soc? Where are you, fella?" Coulter stood very still, listening. There were only night sounds and the smoky aroma of someone barbequing.

Finally, he heard what might be the faint sound of a cat mewing. He hurried down the alley. A huge black cat lay in the gutter. His green eyes were reflected in the light. Coulter reached for the blanket Mary had given him. Soc's eyes were barely open. Blood had matted the fur around his neck. One ear was almost torn off. Soc lifted his head with great effort, then slowly dropped it back to the pavement.

Coulter spread the blanket as he kneeled by the cat.

"Ah, Soc. You've done it this time."

Johnny hurried from the car and held the flashlight as Coulter moved the blanket and gently wrapped Soc into it.

"It must have been a helluva fight," Johnny said.

Coulter talked soothingly as he picked up the cat.

"Hold on, big guy. You'll be okay. Mary's waiting."

He carried Soc to the car and held him as Johnny carefully backed out of the alley.

"You're too old for this shit, Soc." Coulter stroked his head. The cat didn't stir or make a sound as the car moved through the night.

"When did Mary get back?" Johnny asked.

"Yesterday, thank God. She'll fix him up in no time. Knows all the secret Indian remedies." Coulter rubbed the cat's paw. "It's still your territory, big guy, but damn it, you are gonna get killed if you don't stop fighting. You still with me, fella?" He sighed as Soc licked his hand.

Johnny pulled into Coulter's driveway. The porch light was on. No lights showed within. "Come on. Mary's around back," Coulter said.

His aunt, Mary Setting Sun, waited at the open door of the old carriage house. Her black hair, pulled into a long braid, touched the middle of her back. Wisps of gray framed a strong face with a determined chin and a mouth that looked like it smiled a lot. Her black hawk's eyes looked straight into your soul, or so Coulter had always thought. Now they were filled with tenderness, for she also loved the old tomcat.

Coulter breathed in the soothing aroma of cedar and sage as they moved inside. Mary always smoked the carriage house to cleanse it when she returned from one of her journeys.

The one large room was sparsely furnished. An old couch covered with brightly colored Indian blankets also served as a bed. Facing the couch were a well-worn rocking chair and a floor lamp for reading.

A hand-carved oak table and four chairs separated the living area from the kitchen.

"So, Mr. Socrates, you have been fighting again." Mary took the blanket and eased the cat onto the pallet she had prepared on the kitchen table. A myriad of herbs and poultices awaited her patient.

The cat laid perfectly still as Mary quickly and expertly examined him. "It is not as bad as it looks," she announced at last. "Pour yourself and Johnny some coffee. Soc and I will not be long."

"Your usual brew that'll take the paint off a porch?" Johnny laughed.

Coulter made a face. "It's worse than turpentine." He poured two cups from the old speckled pot, which continuously warmed on the woodstove. He handed one to Johnny.

"Guess I can take it if you can," Johnny said.

"It's pretty good when it's first made." Coulter took a sip of the steaming brew and grimaced.

There was no doubt in his mind, Soc would be good as new. He sighed as he leaned back in his chair, set the coffee cup aside, and instantly fell asleep.

13

Coulter lived on White Rock Lake near downtown in the house his father had built in the 1950s. He had added a garden room, which now served as his office. Its glass ceiling gave him the feeling of sitting within the branches of the forty-foot pecan tree which towered above. Two glass walls afforded a magnificent view of the lake.

His office was cluttered with law books, papers, and memorabilia. Two overstuffed chairs faced the carved 18th-century table which served as his desk.

The room was silent except for the sound of a chiming clock, circa 1900, that shared the fireplace mantel with pictures of his now-dead parents and a young, unscarred Socrates.

Coulter watched through the glass ceiling as a squirrel contemplated a jump from one tree limb to another. The leap looked impossible. The squirrel continued to judge the distance, running back and forth, hesitating and making little squirrel chatter. Finally, it leaped effortlessly and landed on the other limb. Coulter decided the squirrel could do this because no one had told him it could not be done.

Bright sunlight streamed through the open French doors leading to the side patio. Clarice parked in the driveway and waited at the patio door until Coulter's attention turned from the papers on his desk.

"You must not have any enemies to sit with your back to the door," she said. "And I refuse to make any jokes about people in glass houses. It's a wonderful room, by the way."

"Hey there, Clarice." He smiled as he got up and pulled out a chair for her. "It's good to see you. It's been too long. I was going to have a glass of wine. Will you join me?"

"Sounds good."

He took a chilled bottle of Chablis from a tiny refrigerator and poured them each a glass.

"It has been a while," Clarice said. "How are you and Soc doing? Is he still fighting every cat on the block?"

He handed her a glass. "And losing. I just drug him out of another alley. Lucky for him, and me, Mary was here to patch him up one more time."

"Mary's back? Good. I've missed her. I'll pop in to say hello before I leave. So, are you working on anything special?"

"A few probates. Nothing earthshaking."

Clarice took a sip of her wine. "I know it's none of my business, but how are you—really?"

He leaned back in his chair. "I still drink, as you can see. Booze wasn't my problem, just my way of avoiding unpleasant memories. I'm getting a handle on my life again, mostly thanks to Mary."

"People grieve in different ways."

"Yeah. Well, tell me, to what do I owe this unexpected pleasure? And may I say, it really is a pleasure."

Clarice grinned. "You're such a charmer. I am damned sure you've heard about the Emily Henderson case?"

He nodded. "The lady who wiped out the two cops. What did the headline say? 'From traffic ticket to capital murder'."

"Horrible headline, and a lie! Anyway, she needs a good lawyer."

Coulter laughed. "I would imagine she does."

He finished his wine, poured another glass for Clarice and a coke for himself. "I would say she needs someone who is up to one hell of a fight. Lowell gets mighty testy over cop killings."

"Yeah. Even Emily's damned husband believes she did it."

Coulter raised one eyebrow. "Well, she obviously has one person on her side."

"We became friends when she was hospitalized after the kidnapping. Emily is a fine young woman, and she is innocent. She went to pieces when the police picked her up after the murders."

"Understandable after what she had already been through. People have cracked under less."

"She doesn't remember much about the night of the murders."

Coulter shook his head. "Whoever defends her has their work cut out for them. It is definitely not a defense attorney's dream."

Clarice picked up the picture of Soc from the mantel. "The reason I'm here—oh hell, Coulter, you've already guessed why I'm here. Would you consider taking her case?"

Coulter stared out at the lake. "Why me?"

"Because you are the best defense attorney in the Southwest."

"Was." He laughed. "How's that for ego? You know I don't take criminal cases anymore."

"Such a waste of talent. Nobody loved a fight more than you." Clarice rushed on. "Damn it, she doesn't have anyone else to turn to."

"I outgrew my savior complex a long time ago. Look--"

The pleading in her eyes stopped him. Clarice Weitzel was not one to beg. He sighed. "Damn it, Clarice, I haven't taken a criminal case in over three years."

"Please, Coulter. I am just asking you to meet her."

"We are talking capital murder, not a traffic citation. She doesn't need a has-been like me."

"You are selling yourself way short. Anyway, can it hurt to meet with her? If you don't want to take her case—fine. Maybe you can suggest someone else."

He smiled. "You're a very persuasive woman. Okay, I'll visit with her— but no promises."

"Thank God. You may be her only hope. She is really desperate."

Coulter chuckled. "That's obvious." His eyes bored into hers. "Before I meet with her, make sure you tell Mrs. Henderson that I have not tried a case in three years and about my drinking problem."

"Your legal vacation and drinking past aren't important."

"Of course they are. I may have lost my edge. I'm not sure I can even try a case again."

"I forgot to mention that she has very little money."

He ruffled her short hair. "Anything else you forgot to mention?"

Clarice smiled. "No. I don't think so."

"Just make sure you explain my background to her. She needs to know the kind of lawyer she's hiring to save her life."

Clarice's cellphone rang. "Excuse me. It's Bannister. I should take it."

She flipped open the phone. "Hey there, Lieutenant." She listened for several minutes, her smile growing.

"What wonderful news. Wait until Lowell hears about this! I'll call you back to plan our celebration."

She closed the phone and turned to Coulter. "This will make all the difference to Emily. I can't wait to tell her. Bannister's been following up on the kidnapping. He questioned patrons at Casa Miguel where Emily was abducted."

"He has two witnesses who saw Hunter and Barnes putting her in the brown car. Both witnesses identified Hunter. Isn't that wonderful?"

"Yes, and no. It will tell the world what bad asses Hunter and Barnes were, and paint a sympathetic picture of Mrs. Henderson as a victim. Unfortunately, it gives her a much stronger motive for killing them."

"You're right, of course. Still, it shows her in a completely different light." Clarice stood up. "Well, with this piece of good news, I'll take my leave. I promise not to pressure you into anything. Whatever you decide about defending her, I won't try to change your mind."

He walked her to her car. "Has a date been set for the prelim?"

"October 20th, I think."

He opened her car door for her. "Just six weeks. Call me after you talk to Mrs. Henderson. If she wants to meet with me, I'll arrange a visit and we'll see how it goes."

"I'm not going to tell you how damned much I appreciate this."
He gave her a hug. "Then don't."

•   •   •   •   •   •   •

Clarice phoned Coulter to bring him up to date. "Dr. Asher says Emily will be fine if we keep her husband away until she's stronger. I just left her at the jail. She was a different woman after I told her about the witnesses. I followed your instructions and she would like very much to meet you."

Coulter grinned as he listened to her. "Okay, okay. I'll set up a meeting."

14

Coulter looked up as Emily Henderson was escorted into the visitors' room. His eyes held hers and he was reminded of Soc's eyes as he had looked up at him from the gutter after his cat fight. He wanted to wrap Emily Henderson in a blanket as he'd done with Soc and take her home for Mary Setting Sun to heal.

He smiled as he held out a chair across from him. "Hello. I'm Coulter McBride," he said, extending his hand.

She hesitated, quickly took it without making eye contact, and as quickly pulled it away. "I'm Emily Henderson."

Her hand was freezing cold in his grip. His father always said to go with your first impression of a client.

Coulter's impression of Emily Henderson? She was scared to death and desperately in need of help.

"Why don't I sit down and we'll visit awhile?" he said, with a smile which extended to his eyes.

Emily watched him take a very old cigarette case from his pocket and open it. She stared at the engraving on the inside.

He followed her gaze.

"It's a snake grasping its tail in its mouth. The endless circle of a person's being. I inherited the case from my father. Like to try one?"

Emily nodded.

He lit a cigarette for her and one for himself.

"Thanks," she said, taking it from him.

He noticed her hand was shaking. "It's okay. The cigarette doesn't obligate you. You don't like me—you don't have to hire me." He realized that in less than five minutes, he had decided to defend her.

Emily took a deep draw on her cigarette and winced, blew out the smoke, and held her ribs as she tried unsuccessfully not to cough. "It tasted wonderful."

He laughed. "How long did you say you've been smoking?"

"It's my ribs. They're taped, and it hurts like crazy when I forget and take a deep breath."

"Sorry. I didn't mean to tease you."

"Don't be sorry," she replied, smiling as best she could. "The taste was worth it."

He leaned back in his chair. His blue eyes were piercing and her gaze dropped under his.

"I'm sure you know the trouble I'm in?"

Coulter chuckled. "Hell, Emily, the whole town knows the trouble you're in!"

Emily frowned for a second, then held her ribs as she laughed. "Touché."

"That was supposed to be kind of an icebreaker. I'm sure Clarice told you about the witnesses Lt. Bannister found who saw you being abducted. It will make a big difference in the murder case."

"I am grateful to Lt. Bannister. He promised to get to the bottom of the assault and he has. Now the people who believed I was lying are proved wrong. I might add that includes my husband," Emily replied, still not looking at him.

"Yeah. Well, first of all, call me Coulter, and feel free to ask me any questions you might have. It is also okay if you don't think you would feel comfortable working with me. There are several top attorneys I can recommend."

Coulter leaned back in his chair. He looked into her eyes. "Clarice filled me in on the details of the assault. Did she tell you about my background?"

"She said you are a top criminal attorney who hasn't taken a case in three years. That I can trust you with my life. You, your aunt Mary and she have been friends for many years. Oh, and she also knew your father. Is there anything else I should know?"

"Did she mention I had a drinking problem in the past?"

"Uh-huh. She said you don't have one now."

Emily got up and walked around the room. "Would you have a problem defending me if you think I'm guilty?"

Coulter shook his head. "I believe anyone at the right time and with the right provocation is capable of murder."

"I think I was capable of murdering Hunter and Barnes."

"You certainly had a powerful motive."

She dropped her head. "Have you ever been wrong about a client? I mean, thought someone was innocent when they were guilty."

"I'm not infallible. I usually get a gut feeling that is seldom wrong."

She began to massage her arm. He knew she wanted to ask how he felt about her guilt or innocence, yet was afraid of his answer.

Emily finally summoned the courage. "Do you have a gut feeling about me?"

"Yeah. I do. I believe you have what is called 'grace under fire'. You have no idea what a strong woman you are. You've been through hell. You were not about to lie half in the river water and half in the mud."

"You clawed your way up and you've been fighting ever since." He took a drag of his cigarette. "But murder—-Nah, you're not capable of killing anyone."

Emily smiled and shook her head. "You do not know how much you saying that means to me. You know, I keep asking myself why you would consider taking my case. Clarice said it would be your first criminal defense case in three years. It can't be for money. I don't have any."

"Actually, I surprised myself. Maybe it's because my life was shattered not so long ago and with help, I've worked through it." Coulter took off his jacket. "So, why don't you tell me a little about yourself, Emily?"

"Why don't you tell me a little about yourself, Coulter? I don't feel much like talking just now."

"Fair enough. I'm half Cherokee and half Irish. My grandfather was a lawyer, the same as my father and me. My father married a beautiful Cherokee lady, Crystal Evening Star. She passed to the other side when I was born, so my aunt, Mary Setting Sun, raised me. I love the law and a reprobate of fur known as Socrates--my brilliant feline."

"Clarice mentioned your aunt Mary. I think Clarice said she's a shaman."

"Yes, she is. Her full name is Mary Setting Sun."

"Why didn't you include Mary in who or what you love?"

He picked up his cigarette. "What is this?" He laughed. "Am I being interrogated?"

Emily's face flushed. "I don't know why I asked."

"It must be the Cherokee in me. There are people and certain things that are beyond love. They are part of your soul. Mary Setting Sun is part of my soul. Haven't you ever felt that way about anyone or anything?"

She looked down at the table. "Yes—once—a long time ago."

"Then you know what I mean. Many criminal defense lawyers are heavy drinkers—occupational hazard. I certainly was. A colleague once said a good criminal defense attorney is totally callous or a drunk." He looked at her keenly. "I was drunk for a year. That's behind me now—at least I hope it is. I wanted you to know the chance you might be taking if you decide to hire me to represent you."

Emily smiled at him. "Aren't you taking a chance on me?"

Coulter shrugged. "Not the same thing. You don't have a lot of time to choose your attorney. The preliminary hearing is in six weeks and there is a lot of investigation to be done."

"I think I've already made my decision."

"Well, my father thought it was a good idea to sleep on it before making any major decision. So let's both sleep on it and we'll visit tomorrow. A trial is never easy. You'll need to remember a lot of details. I'll bring you a notebook so you can jot down anything you remember, no matter how insignificant it may seem. It will be helpful to any attorney you might choose."

Emily began rubbing her arm again. He was afraid of pushing her too far and decided to wrap it up.

As he stood, she looked up at him. "Remembering is my problem, Coulter. The night of the murders is pretty much a blank I haven't been able to fill in."

Coulter touched her shoulder. "Don't worry about it. You'll be surprised at the details which come back to you when you have an opportunity to take it step by step. I'll show you what I mean when I come back tomorrow."

Emily walked over and pressed the button for the matron. "You are exactly the way Clarice described you." She held out her hand. "Thank you for coming. I'll see you tomorrow."

15

The following day Emily was led into Parkland Hospital's security ward visitors' room. Coulter was already inside.

"Did you get some rest?" he asked.

"Uh, huh. I am so grateful to Mr. Lowell for moving me from the jail. It's a wonderful program he's started. Prisoners who are awaiting trial and are suffering from physical or mental problems are brought here, away from the general jail population." She rushed on. "Well, I've slept on it. I still want you for my attorney. What about you?"

"Yeah, I want to represent you. So I expect we should get to work." Colter took out his tape recorder. "I hope this doesn't bother you. I still take notes. It's possible to miss something important, and the recorder is my backup."

"Sure. No problem."

"Okay. Let's work backward and see what you remember. Describe your arrest."

"I came home at nine o'clock on Tuesday morning. Two police officers were waiting to take me downtown for questioning. I tried to run away—which was a big mistake!"

"Why did you go home? Didn't you realize the police would have the house staked out?"

"Of course not. I did not know Hunter and Barnes were dead."

He was pleased with her answer. "Did you have a weapon?"

Emily nodded. "I took a .38 caliber pistol and bullets from home to Clarice's lake house."

His eyes widened. "Where is the gun now?"

"I thought it was in my car, but the police didn't find it."

"You have no idea where it is?"

"No."

"Why did you take a gun with you?"

"I was afraid."

Coulter watched her reaction as he spoke. "You know, I'd have a good chance of getting you off if you did kill them."

"I admit I wished them dead. I even dreamed of killing them." Her voice faded as she looked past him. "The last thing I recall is waking from a nightmare about them.

"Bits and pieces of what they did to me started flashing through my mind. I couldn't handle it and drank some brandy, which apparently didn't mix well with my pain pills. The next thing I knew, I was getting out of my car in front of my house."

"What time was that, again?"

"Around nine in the morning. The police were waiting. They told me Hunter and Barnes were dead. I laughed. I guess I was hysterical. My memory sort of faded out and when it faded back in again, I was in jail. They told me I signed a confession."

"The police were staking out your house since four a.m. Your husband arrived a little while after. Any idea where he might have spent the night?"

Emily shrugged. "None at all."

"Was he in the habit of staying out all night?"

"He travels a great deal. He didn't go with me to the dinner because he always goes dove hunting on the first day of the season. He had planned to stay the weekend, but didn't because of what happened to me. I don't know why he would have been out all night."

Emily began to rub her arm again. It was already red. Coulter made a note to have Clarice mention it to the shrink. She apparently rubbed her arms when she became upset or felt under pressure.

"I don't believe I could have killed them," Emily said, "but my memory lapse is frightening. I'm afraid of what I may have done in those lost hours."

"During my drunk year, I had a few memory blanks myself," Coulter confided. "You may have slept the entire time. We'll track down those missing hours. Then we'll know exactly what we are dealing with. Now stop worrying. It may turn out you have an alibi. If you are innocent, we'll get you acquitted. If you're guilty, we may still get you acquitted."

"What are you saying?" Emily looked as if she were going to cry.

"When the jury realizes you were half out of your mind after Hunter and Barnes kidnapped and tried to kill you—if their murders were not premeditated—and most importantly, when we show them that Hunter and Barnes were real bastards who needed killing, they may very well vote to acquit. It's the Texas brand of 'justifiable homicide'. 'They needed killin'."

Emily shook her head. "That is the most ridiculous thing I have ever heard."

Coulter smiled. "Maybe, but it's happened before. The most important thing a client and their lawyer have going for them is complete honesty. You have to trust me and you have to be honest with me. You must tell me the absolute truth, no matter how bad you may think it is. I give you my word. I will tell you the truth every step of the way."

Emily smiled. "I knew I could trust you the moment you came through the door. I promise you will get nothing but the truth from me." She hesitated. But there is one problem. I don't know how I will be able to pay you."

"That's not important."

"I have some money of my own. It's in a trust fund my grandfather set up. I don't think there is very much in it. You can have whatever there is. I have no intention of being a charity case."

"We can settle up when it's over and you're free."

Emily smiled. "So, this is how criminal defense attorneys usually work? You must have been very good not to worry about getting paid upfront. If I'm not freed, somehow I will make sure you are paid."

Coulter gently touched her arm. "Don't worry. You are going to go free. Forget about the damned money. The only important thing is getting you off. I am sure Lowell will insist on you being examined by his psychiatrist to stave off an insanity plea on our part."

Emily didn't make any comment.

Coulter looked as if he were deciding whether to say something as he held her gaze for a long time. "I want you to think about what I'm going to tell you with an open mind. As I said, Lowell will have you examined by a shrink. It is imperative for you to recover those missing hours."

"I know."

"My aunt, Mary Setting Sun, is a full-blooded Cherokee Indian. Mary is also a shaman."

"A shaman is a medicine man or woman, is that right?"

Coulter nodded. "Right. I think Mary might help you find those lost hours."

Emily was thoughtful for a moment. "You have a lot of faith in her, don't you?"

"Yes. You'll see why if you decide to meet her."

"I would like to meet her. Of course, she may not want to deal with a suspected murderer."

"You couldn't be more wrong. Mary is the only completely non-judgmental person I have ever known. She looks straight into your heart and sees the truth."

Emily looked him in the eye. "I'm not afraid of Mary's analysis. I can't wait to meet her."

"Good. I'll talk to her tonight. One other thing. There is no chance the judge will grant bail in a capital murder case. I'm afraid you're here at Parkland for the duration."

"I don't mind. If I were out, I would have to deal with Dan."

"Dan's your husband?"

Emily nodded.

"I got the impression from Clarice that he's not very supportive."

"That's an understatement. Dan believes I am a murderer."

"Sorry—must be tough to take."

Coulter could see behind her apparent calm, Emily was becoming agitated again. He decided not to push her to talk any further.

"I have to start some investigations rolling. I'll fill Mary in and make arrangements for her to meet you." He got up to ring for the matron.

"I appreciate everything you are doing for me." Emily choked up as tears came into her eyes. "I can't imagine what I would have done if you had refused to defend me."

Coulter started to put his arm around her, caught himself, and reached for her hand instead. "You'd probably have found someone better. Remember—we are in this together and we are going to win."

With an effort, Emily regained her composure. "I'll remember." She put her other hand over his, then stared at their hands, surprised at herself. She had not wanted to touch anyone with affection in a long time.

Coulter watched her as the matron opened the door. Emily walked out of the room with her head held high. Her body was no longer drooping with her previous air of defeat. Coulter suspected that, for the first time, Emily Henderson felt strong enough to fight.

16

It was storming when Coulter arrived home. The door to the carriage house was open to let in the sound and smell of the rain.

"Hey, Mary," he called from the doorway.

"You are just in time for dinner," she replied.

It felt so comfortable inside, Coulter thought. A fire crackled in the fireplace. Mary was at the wooden cookstove stirring a pot of some kind.

The inevitable coffee pot was perking on the back burner.

"I am glad for your company. Just warming up some chili and cornbread," Mary said.

Coulter laughed. "Hell, Mary, you can't cook. Where did you get the chili?"

She tried to look indignant, gave up, and grinned instead. "If you must know, it was a gift."

He watched his aunt set the table. She moved so gracefully, not a wasted or hurried movement. The aroma of cedar blended with that of the drying herbs. As always, a sense of peace filled the room.

Coulter waited as Mary offered a prayer of thanks for their food. He took one spoonful of the chili and reached for his water. "Whoever made this chili must love jalapenos," he said. "They redeemed themselves with this wonderful sweet cornbread."

Mary continued eating in silence. When they finished, she cleared the table and poured their coffee.

"Clarice asked me to see Emily Henderson. She's the lady who's charged with the capital murder of the two police officers."

Mary nodded. Her eyes looked dreamy. Coulter knew she was concentrating on his voice and "seeing" him.

"I've decided to defend her."

Mary nodded. "Did you use your tape recorder during your talks?"

"Uh-huh."

"And you want me to meet her?"

Coulter nodded. "I thought you could help her remember the ten or eleven hours between around ten o'clock in the evening and nine o'clock the next morning."

"I would like to hear her voice from your tape."

Coulter smiled. "You want to listen to my confidential conversation?"

"Quit your teasing. I merely want to hear her speak a word or two, so I can visualize her."

"I'll get the tape."

Coulter retrieved the recorder from his briefcase as Mary cleared the dishes.

He set it on the table between them and turned it on. They heard Emily say, "Sure. No problem."

Mary nodded. "That is enough."

It was several minutes before she spoke. "I will meet Emily Henderson. The day after tomorrow will be good."

"Thanks, Mary. If anyone can help her regain her memory, it's you. I've talked to Lowell. He has moved her to Parkland. It's one of his new projects to confine prisoners who are physically or mentally impaired to the hospital."

"Yes, I know," Mary replied.

17

Coulter took the freight elevator to the top of the downtown warehouse where Johnny Tompkins lived and worked. Coulter opened the door marked JOHNNY TOMPKINS INVESTIGATIONS.

A middle-aged blonde with a beehive hairdo peered at him over rimless half-glasses. Her smile softened her entire face, its sweetness making her look years younger than her sixty-odd years. "Hi, there, Coulter. Go on in. He's not busy."

He returned her smile. "Thanks, Irene."

Johnny Tompkins' feet were propped up on a massive oak desk, revealing highly-polished cowboy boots. The ever-present Stetson was tipped back on his head. His long, rangy body was clad in his usual western shirt and faded Levis.

Country and western music blared from a radio. His face broke into a craggy grin as he switched it off. "Hey there, buddy. How's the world treatin' ya?"

Coulter laughed. "Your drawl gets thicker every time I see you."

"Yeah, ain't it a honey?"

Coulter plopped down in a chair across from Johnny's desk. Without moving his feet, Johnny reached into a drawer and brought out a fifth of

Wellers bourbon. He unscrewed the top and handed the bottle to Coulter, who took a long drink.

"Ahh, I really needed that."

"You do look a might tuckered," Johnny said.

Coulter tried to sound nonchalant. "I've hired on in the Henderson case."

"Better have another drink. You sure don't pick the easy ones."

"The easy ones aren't any fun."

Coulter took another drink from the bottle and passed it back.

"Whadda you think of your client?" Johnny asked.

"Controlled hysteria."

"Yeah?"

"Emily Henderson is tough. Still, I think she is about one step away from losing it completely. Shrinks call it post-traumatic stress disorder. I call it having more dumped on you than anyone could handle."

"She has been through a little bit."

"Yeah, she has. Pass me the bottle. It may be my last drink until the trial's over."

"Don't do nothin' hasty." Johnny took a drink and passed it back. "You want me to do a little snoopin'?"

"I need the police reports on Mrs. Henderson's case and the murders, of course. I also want everything on Hunter and Barnes — background, friends, enemies—the works."

"Somebody out there was sure mad at them two. It hurts just to think of where she shot 'em."

"It might be someone with a grudge who they helped send up."

"There's plenty of women mean enough to have done it. I've met a few of 'em myself."

Coulter chuckled. "Possibly in those shit-kickin' joints where you hang out."

"Yes sir, some of those gals get pretty tough from bein' pushed around by them rednecks. Kinda woman I like—afraid of nothing, high spirited, and loving."

Coulter laughed. It occurred to him it had been a long time since he'd laughed. "I want to know everything about Emily Henderson. The husband's interesting. We will also zero in on him. I don't think we're going to like him."

Johnny grinned. "Yep, we're back in harness again. Just like old times."

Coulter stood up to go. "I didn't realize I missed it so much. Thanks for the Wellers."

"My pleasure, counselor. What are your chances of getting her off?"

Coulter sighed. "It sure as hell doesn't look good." He grinned. "But then, it ain't over with yet."

18

It took a week of telephone calls before Dan Henderson consented to a meeting.

He had suggested meeting at Coulter's office. The appointment was for six o'clock and Henderson was already thirty minutes late. When the bell rang, Coulter answered the door himself. The two men eyed each other like two fighters—each sizing up the other.

"Mr. Henderson? I'm Coulter McBride," he said, offering his hand. "Come on in."

Dan ignored Coulter's hand. "Pretty fancy house," he remarked as they walked through the living room and into Coulter's office. He frowned as he spotted Clarice sitting on the couch furthest from Coulter's desk.

"I think you've already met Mrs. Weitzel," he said. "She will take notes."

Clarice nodded. "Hello, Mr. Henderson."

Dan ignored her. "I thought I was just going to be talking to you," he said, turning to Coulter.

"Clarice and I are old friends. I'm short a secretary right now. She has kindly volunteered to help with your wife's case."

Dan took the chair across from Coulter and drummed his fingers impatiently on the desk. "So, you're my wife's lawyer." He leaned back in his chair and lit a cigarette. "I was ready to hire the best. She wouldn't have it. I think she made a big mistake."

"I would like to ask you a few questions, if you don't mind, Mr. Henderson."

"Fire away."

"How would you describe your wife's emotional state after the assault?"

"Really paranoid. Couldn't sleep. Popped a bunch of pills."

"Are you suggesting she was emotionally unstable?" Coulter asked.

"I'm not sure what you mean by 'emotionally unstable'. She was pretty messed up. Like I said, she was high on pain pills all the time. Man, she really got upset when I wouldn't let her file charges. Guess she wanted to prove to me that she was telling the truth."

Coulter's eyes narrowed. "Why would she need to prove anything to you?"

Dan shrugged. "Who the hell knows?"

"Could it be she felt you didn't believe her story about the kidnapping?"

"You have to admit her story was pretty far-fetched. Still, I guess she was telling the truth after all."

Coulter didn't try to hide his irritation. "What do you mean?" he snapped.

"The two cops are dead, aren't they?"

"Mr. Henderson, do you think your wife murdered Hunter and Barnes?"

"Sure. Don't you?"

Coulter walked over to the mantle. "No, Mr. Henderson. I am certain your wife is innocent."

"I guess a lawyer has to pretend to believe his client is innocent, whether he does or not. Gotta collect those fees. Course, in this case, she doesn't have any money to pay you."

Coulter resisted the impulse to slap the smirk off his face. He glanced at Clarice. Her head was bent over her shorthand pad. He noticed the knuckles of the hand gripping her ballpoint pen were white.

"Mr. Henderson," Coulter continued in a calm voice, "the police arrived at your home around four a.m. and arrested your wife when she arrived at nine. They say you didn't arrive home until after five. Where were you all night, if you don't mind my asking?"

Dan gave him a knowing look. "Obviously I wasn't at home."

Coulter's face was expressionless. "No kidding."

"I have an alibi, if that's what you're wondering."

"She got a name?"

"What the hell. You're gonna find out from Bannister, anyway. It's Wanda Sikorsky."

"Where can I find her?"

"Do I have to draw you a map, shyster? Ah, hell, she manages the Tumble Inn out on Harry Hines."

Coulter could no longer contain himself. "You know, Dan, you are one sorry son of a bitch!"

Dan bolted from his chair and sputtered with anger. "I don't have to put up with that kind of talk from a shyster lawyer like you."

Coulter waited, hoping Dan would take a swing at him, but he only turned on his heel and stormed out the patio door.

Clarice sighed. "Dan Henderson is a real piece of work."

"Yeah. He sure is. I can't believe Emily could have married him."

Clarice gave him a funny look, but didn't reply.

· · · · ·

Johnny stuck his head in through the patio door. "Hey, ya'll. Wasn't that ole Dan Henderson I just passed outside?"

"Uh-huh. Want a drink?" Coulter replied.

"What was the sombitch so puffed up about?"

Clarice nodded her head in response to Coulter's questioning look. He poured her a shot of Black Jack and handed it to her, along with a can of Millers.

Coulter laughed. "I don't think Mr. Henderson likes me."

"How did the hearing go this morning?" Johnny asked.

"About like I expected. Judge Pernett agreed to Lowell's request for a psychiatrist for Emily. I asked for a speedy trial date. Lowell wants one, too. We have another six weeks to prepare our defense."

"Guess I better get crackin'. How is Mr. District Attorney these days? Old Lowell will try the case personally, I bet."

"With the election only three months away, you know he will," Clarice replied. "Unfortunately for him, he's going to lose. He just doesn't know it yet. If he did, he would try to get it postponed until after the election."

Coulter stretched back in his chair. "I've been doing some thinking about the why, where, when, and who. There are sure a lot of questions that need answering." Coulter pulled a notepad from the pile of papers on his desk and began to read.

"Why Emily Henderson? Was it simply chance, or was it planned?

"If it was a coincidence, were Hunter and Barnes just out for some fun, or did they intend to kill her all along so she couldn't talk? Did they know who she was? I can't believe they just drove by the West-End Steakhouse, saw a woman come out, and kidnapped her. It would have been too chancy. I don't think they were stupid.

"If it was planned, who was behind it?" Coulter stopped to get his breath and refill their glasses, taking a coke for himself.

"Who had a motive?" Coulter continued. "Husband? Lover? Husband's lover, assuming he had only one. What enemies did Emily have? What about enemies of her husband? A guy like him is bound to have more than his share. He says he was with Wanda Sikorsky all night."

Coulter looked up from his notes. "Johnny, Mrs. Henderson mentioned something about a trust fund. She was a little vague about it. We need to find out how much is in it."

Coulter began to read again. "If someone wanted Emily Henderson dead, is there a connection between that person and the policemen?"

Johnny nodded. "You're right, there might be a whole lot goin' on."

"Why were the policemen killed?" Coulter continued. "Who had a motive? Was the killer or killers only after one cop, but killed both to make it look like Emily did it?"

Johnny took off his hat and scratched his head. "Well, of course they could a killed either man somewhere else without the second man bein' around. I think the killer decided it was perfect to kill them both and set Emily Henderson up to take the fall."

Coulter glanced at Clarice. "What do you think?"

"She was the perfect patsy. But how could they know Emily wouldn't have an alibi?"

"Good point." Counter continued. "Were the cops hired to kill Emily? Did the killer act because Hunter and Barnes muffed the job, or because the killer had to keep Hunter and Barnes quiet about who hired them?"

"Or were the murders totally unrelated to Emily and just a coincidence?" Clarice interjected.

"If the murders were premeditated and calculated to put the blame on Emily, again, how did the killer know she wouldn't have an alibi? Did the killer know about Emily's movements, or was she just lucky? Maybe the killer had a confederate watching Emily." Coulter threw the pad back on the desk and drank the rest of his coke.

Johnny's eyes squinted shut. "Or there is the other possibility. Did Emily Henderson murder the policemen?"

"Yeah, I guess we can't rule that out," Coulter replied. "There is a lot she doesn't remember. We've got to fill in those blanks."

"I got a line on Barnes," Johnny said.

"Oh, yeah? What about him?" Coulter asked.

"He had a roommate, name's Nancy Osborne. She's agreed to see you this evening at about eight. She didn't want to talk to me."

Coulter glanced at his watch. "How about it, guys? I'll spring for dinner at El Fenix before heading over to see Ms. Osborne."

"Gotta pass. I'm late already. Catch you two later," Johnny said, heading for the door.

After he had gone, Coulter turned to Clarice. "So, how about a little Tex-Mex?"

"There's something I need to talk with you about."

"Can't we discuss it over dinner?"

"No. I had better tell you now before I lose my nerve."

"Sounds serious."

Clarice ran her hand through her hair. "Bannister called me the morning of the murders. He told me about the murders, and that he was looking for Emily."

"Yeah?"

"I told him I didn't know where she was. After we hung up, I drove to the lake house to warn her. She was gone." Clarice took a deep breath. "So I drove to her house. There was no sign of her, though her car was in the driveway. I searched the car and found her gun." Clarice hesitated, then forced herself to go on. "I took the gun and dropped it in a storm drain near the Center."

"You what!"

"Coulter, I panicked. I know—I know it was a stupid thing to do. I was sure Emily had killed them. I only wanted to protect her."

"Did you even check to see if someone had fired the gun?"

Clarice shook her head. "I am so sorry."

He sighed as he stood up. "There's nothing we can do about it now. Come on, let's get something to eat."

"No," she replied, "I just want to go home. Call me later if you find out anything new."

"Sure." He hugged her. "Don't worry about it, Clarice."

19

The door of the house on Lee Avenue opened in response to Coulter's knock.

Nancy Osborne stood silhouetted in the light. She wore a short blue terrycloth robe open almost to the waist. Her protruding spidery white arms and legs seemed obscene. Or perhaps, Coulter thought, they just made her seem more naked.

Nancy's gaze started at Coulter's expressionless face and moved slowly down his body.

"My, my, what have we here?" she purred.

There was no mistaking her predatory look, nor the fact that she was stoned.

"Ms. Osborne?"

"Um, hum."

"I'm Emily Henderson's lawyer, Coulter McBride. My investigator said you were expecting me."

Nancy held the door open and motioned him inside with a wide sweep of her arm, which, Coulter feared, would cause the robe to open the rest of the way.

She smiled as she looked him up and down. "Um, hum. Come right on in."

Coulter followed her into the overdressed living room.

Nancy picked up her joint, took a long drag, and offered it to him.

Coulter shook his head. "I understand you and Philip Barnes were roommates."

"For three years. But he was moving out."

"Mind if I ask why?"

"I know it's a cliché—but Philip had become a bore. He didn't make much money, and as you can see, I have expensive taste." Nancy's eyes held his. "Do you make lots of money, Coulter? Okay if I call you Coulter?"

"Sure." He glanced around the room at the obviously expensive furniture and wondered who had footed the bill. "If you don't mind my asking, Ms. Osborne."

"Please call me Nancy."

"Tell me, Nancy, what line of work are you in that you can afford all of this lovely furniture?"

Nancy preened, obviously pleased at what she thought was a compliment.

"You might say I am an artist, Coulter. I ferret out old hidden treasures and restore them into beautiful antiques. Philip helped financially when he could. As you can see, I am remodeling the house and that costs money."

"I didn't realize policemen made that kind of money. Was Barnes independently wealthy?"

"Heavens no. He did odd jobs from time to time."

"Oh, what kind of odd jobs?" Coulter asked, trying to sound nonchalant.

"I never asked him. Of course, his sister is very rich."

Coulter raised an eyebrow. "I was not aware he had a sister."

"Oh, yes. Little Marcia. She is married to a very wealthy man."

"Do you happen to know where she lives?"

Nancy smiled at him. "Um, hmm. Buddy Lambert has a fabulous house in Parkview. I've sold him several pieces."

"Did Barnes have any enemies you know of?"

"Well, his sister, of course." Nancy kept shaking her leg. Luckily, the robe thus far had not fallen open. Coulter tried to avert his gaze.

"Why do you say that?" he asked.

"Because Philip was blackmailing her. And before you ask, I have no idea what he had on her. Whatever it was, it must have been really good."

"Anyone else who might have a motive for killing him?"

"Really, Coulter, whoever killed Philip, also killed Hunter. I'd say that rather narrows the field to your client."

"Did Barnes tell you he kidnapped Mrs. Henderson?"

Nancy took her time putting a cigarette into an ebony holder, then lit it with a gold Dunhill lighter. She carefully blew several smoke rings before answering. "Among others. Philip was a very violent man, and he loved to brag."

Coulter leaned forward. "What do you mean—others?"

"Mrs. Henderson was not the first, you know. Philip and his partner had played their little game before."

Coulter wondered why Nancy was volunteering all this information. Maybe it was some kind of ego trip, or revenge, or maybe she was just running off at the mouth because she was stoned.

"With who?" Coulter asked quickly. It would be a big break for Emily if there was another woman who could testify against Hunter and Barnes.

"Well, let me see, there was this young nurse. That was a few years ago." Nancy crushed out her cigarette. "Of course, she wasn't as lucky as your client."

Coulter frowned. "What do you mean?"

"I mean, they killed her."

"They what!"

"They killed her. Yeah, it was a while back. Philip had just moved in with me." She smiled. "Things were really great back at the beginning. Philip said he and Hunter were hired to do a job. This young nurse was at the wrong place at the wrong time and saw the whole thing. They had to get rid of her."

Coulter was momentarily speechless, as his mind. It wasn't possible. Yet there couldn't be such a coincidence.

"Do you remember the woman's name?" Coulter asked at last. Somehow, he knew what Nancy's answer would be.

"It was like pretzel. No. It was Weitzel. Yes, Laurie Weitzel. I saved the clippings if you would like to see them."

Coulter could only stare at her. "Yes, I would."

Nancy left the room. When she came back, she handed him some yellowed newspaper clippings in a plastic cover. He simply could not believe it. After all this time, Clarice would know who had murdered her daughter. An odd thought occurred to him. What if she already knew?

Nancy mistook Coulter's look of incredulity. "You find it hard to understand my attraction to someone so violent, don't you? Well, there is something infinitely exciting about being with someone you know is capable of murder."

Coulter regained his voice. "Why would Barnes tell you about Laurie Weitzel?"

"Lovers whisper strange things to each other, especially when they're high." She stood up. "Look, I would like to have you stay, but unfortunately, I'm expecting company."

She walked with him to the door and rested her hand on his arm. "It's too bad company's coming. We could have a lot of fun together. Please come back again, Coulter. Anytime you want."

"I may do that. You've been very helpful, Nancy. Thank you."

He breathed a sigh as she closed the door behind him. Should he tell Clarice what he had discovered? Probably not until he had thoroughly checked it out.

Nancy could have been lying, yet why would she keep the article otherwise? He made a mental note to dig out old police records.

Then a disturbing thought crossed his mind. Could Clarice have somehow discovered Hunter and Barnes killed Laurie and had taken her revenge? She knew Emily wouldn't have an alibi for Monday night. This case was beginning to be like peeling an onion. You peeled off a layer, and you just came to another one. He wondered what he would find at the center.

20

"Bannister," came the voice at the other end of the line.

"How about scampi—one o'clock?"

"I'm not talking about the Henderson case, McBride."

"This is another matter."

"See you there."

• • • • •

Coulter entered the semi-darkness of Campisi's Lounge. He'd always wondered why the sign outside added 'Egyptian Lounge'. No one ever called the restaurant anything except Campisi's. It had been the Italian restaurant forever.

The original restaurant was long and narrow with five 1950s vinyl booths on the right side—some with slits that only added to their authenticity. There was a doorway leading to another small room, then another booth at the very back. To the left of it was the long bar.

April smiled and motioned Coulter to his usual booth at the back. He breathed in the wonderful aroma of garlic and tomato sauce, homemade Italian sausage, and the faint aroma of stale beer. The walls were lined with autographed pictures of famous customers who never missed a visit to Campisi's when they were in town.

Bannister arrived at exactly one o'clock and sat down in the booth opposite him. He smiled his thanks as April set down their Miller drafts.

"You both want your usual?" April asked.

Both men nodded.

"So, you're back in the game, mouthpiece?"

"Looks that way, flatfoot."

They sipped their beers. It was understood there would be no conversation until they had eaten.

April brought them salads and hot, crisp garlic bread. The shrimp scampi, one of Campisi's signature dishes, was served in a stainless-steel bowl with crusty parmesan and breadcrumbs covering succulent shrimp, which lay in an incredibly seasoned garlic sauce. April brought plain Italian bread for dipping up the sauce, along with spaghetti with homemade Italian sausage for Coulter, and a pizza with everything, including anchovies for Bannister.

Halfway through their meal, Coulter signaled for two more Millers.

Both men, totally sated, leaned back in contentment.

"What's on your mind?" Bannister asked at last.

"I came across an interesting situation—something you might be interested in."

"And you want a favor."

"Yes, and no." Coulter recounted his conversation with Nancy Osborne and handed Bannister copies of the clippings.

Bannister quickly looked them over.

"I thought you might want to check out the DNA from Laurie's murder to see if there is a match."

Bannister chewed on his cigar. "To put your mind at ease, Clarice didn't waste them. She and I talked about a possible match. I'm way ahead of you, as usual. DNA results should be back in a couple of days. There wasn't anything else to tie the two crimes together until you got the Osborne dame to talk. Glad to see you've been doing your homework."

"If there's a match, she'll finally get the closure she's needed for so long," Coulter said. "Selfishly, it will be an advantage to Emily Henderson at trial. One she deserves."

"It'll take a few more days," Bannister said. "I'll let you and Lowell know the results. I'd like to be the one to tell Clarice, if you don't mind."

Coulter nodded. "Sure."

Bannister scooted out of the booth. "Thanks for lunch. You know I like the kid. It is about time she got a break."

21

Coulter stood up as Emily walked into Parkland's visitors' room. She looked agitated. He didn't have long to wonder why.

"Dan came by to see me."

"I met with him briefly yesterday," Coulter replied.

"What did you think of him?"

Coulter shrugged, decided not to hedge. "I thought he was an obnoxious jerk." He smiled. "That's the cleaned-up version."

"I have asked him for a divorce." Emily's chin came up as if she expected him to challenge her decision.

"I'm not sure that is such a wise idea." Yet he realized he was pleased.

"Dan says he will fight it. That makes no sense at all. Why would he want to stay married? Especially when he believes I'm a murderer."

"Maybe in his own way, he loves you."

Emily's laugh sounded bitter even to her own ears. "He said if we weren't married, they could force him to testify against me."

"Yes. That's true."

"He doesn't know anything that could hurt me."

"Maybe he thinks he does. I'll find out whatever he thinks he knows."

"I shouldn't ask you." She hesitated for a moment. "Would you consider handling the divorce for me?"

"Emily, it would be best to wait to file for divorce until after the trial for several reasons."

"Name one?"

"The divorce is bound to affect you and I don't want you having even more stress to deal with. I think a murder trial is quite enough."

"I'll be more stressed out if I have to stay married to Mr. Dan Henderson!"

Coulter shrugged. "If you're sure it's what you want, I'll handle it. It won't be final until after the trial, anyway. It takes sixty days after filing before a divorce decree is granted. By the way, your appointment with Dr. Hastings-Frost is tomorrow morning."

"Who?"

"The psychiatrist who Marshall Lowell, the District Attorney, is having examine you. Clarice is checking with the matron to see if she can bring you some of your own clothes for the meeting."

Emily frowned. "Why should Clarice want to help me? She hardly knows me."

"To begin with, her daughter Laurie was kidnapped and murdered. We now think by Hunter and Barnes. It's the same M.O."

"I remember now. She told me about her daughter when I was in the hospital. What does this have to do with me?"

"Clarice has made the Women's Crisis Center her whole life—helping women in similar situations. You also happen to bear an uncanny resemblance to her daughter."

"Sorry. Guess I'm suspicious of everyone's motives today."

"You're entitled to be a little paranoid."

She smiled at him. "Got a cigarette for your nut case?"

He pulled the cigarette case from his pocket and lit cigarettes for them both.

"We got special dispensation to smoke in here. Lowell had it okayed."

"Oh. Thanks."

She braced herself for the pain in her ribs. "I gotta quit smoking anyway before it kills me." She laughed. "Unless something else kills me first."

Coulter grinned. "Not funny."

"Well, tomorrow we will see just how crazy I really am." She realized she was handling things a lot better. She could even joke about her situation.

Coulter smiled. "I don't think you're crazy."

"Does that mean you won't plead me temporarily insane?" She watched closely for his reaction.

"I've already pled you not guilty—period."

"Is it still what you believe?"

"Yes, it is."

She sighed. "Thank you."

"Mary Setting Sun also thinks you are innocent, and she is never wrong."

Emily felt a sudden twinge of jealousy. "Who is Mary Setting Sun again?"

Coulter propped his feet up on the table. "She's my aunt, remember?"

"Oh, of course." She felt foolish for her moment of jealousy. "Why don't you tell me more about your life? After all, tomorrow I'll be telling the shrink all about mine." Emily tried to make her voice light, but she wanted to know everything there was to know about Coulter McBride.

He lit another cigarette. "My grandfather, Patrick McBride, came from Ireland as a kid, along with his mother.

"They went to the Oklahoma territory during the great land rush of 1893. His mother's dream was that Patrick become a lawyer. I won't bore you with the details. Before he was twenty years old, he had done time—for a crime he didn't commit. Eventually, he was pardoned and went on to become a lawyer. They say he was the best damned lawyer in Oklahoma. He had one son—my father."

"Dad fought it out for the Indians when oil was king and everyone wanted to steal it from them. He told me a lot of stories about those days. I live in the house he brought my mother to as a bride. I have a lot to remind me of my heritage. I am very proud of it.

"Mary Setting Sun is my mother's sister. If the Court would allow it, Mary would be talking to you tomorrow instead of Dr. Hastings-Frost. Mary is uncanny. She sees straight into your heart. I spoke to her about you.

She'll be coming by to meet you in a couple of days." He sighed, "So, anyway, now you know a little more about me."

"Are you married?"

He laughed. "No. Only to the law. I've been thinking seriously of getting a divorce."

"What happened to your father?" she asked.

It was as if a curtain fell over his eyes. "That's another story. I'll tell you about it sometime." He stood up to leave.

Damn, Emily thought, why did I have to pry? She had picked up before that Coulter's father was somehow a touchy subject. He talked about his father with such love. She started for the door. I would give anything to find out who my father was. She wished for the hundredth time.

22

Coulter took a long, hot shower. The events of the day had made him feel like he needed another one.

When he finally felt clean, he dressed in turtleneck and slacks, made himself a drink, and stretched out on the couch. The telephone rang almost immediately. It was Johnny. Coulter quickly filled him in on the interviews.

"What have you found out about Laurie Weitzel?" Coulter asked.

"The M.O. is similar. She was kidnapped and shot in the head with a .38."

"I remember they also found her in the Trinity River Bottoms," Coulter said.

"Yeah. Course, they find a lot a people in the Trinity River Bottoms."

"True," Coulter replied.

"She'd been on the 3-11 shift at the hospital. Barnes and Hunter were workin' together then, too. They were also workin' nights. That's all I've got so far."

"It's a good start."

"Coulter, this case's gettin' a little complicated."

"I know. I couldn't believe it when Nancy showed me the newspaper clippings. Of course, we only have her word for it.

"Hold on a second." Coulter lit a cigarette. "I've given it a lot of thought and I don't think there is any way Clarice could have suspected Hunter and Barnes murdered her daughter. What might have happened was that after they kidnapped Emily, the similarities were so strong, they could have overwhelmed her." He sighed. "No, damn it, I've known Clarice too long. She is just not capable of murder."

"You know what you always say, 'anybody's capable of murder if the timing's right'."

"Don't remind me. You don't need to check on her. She already pretty much told me about her movements."

"Gotcha. By the way, I've been checkin' on the Hendersons. They've got a little over $800 in their joint checking account and $2,000 in a savings account. Mrs. Henderson's life insurance is for $10,000. Hardly enough to kill over.

"I've got a copy of the tax returns. About the trust she spoke of, all the money is from mineral rights her granddaddy, who was a surveyor, took as payment for his services. There's about $1,800.00 in it now."

Coulter frowned. "Mineral rights?"

"Yeah."

"Are the lessees listed on the returns?" Coulter asked.

Johnny flipped through the pages. "Yeah. Let's see, there's Sun Oil and Phillips and some others."

"Is there any way you can get a list of what and where the properties are?"

"No problem. I'll get 'em."

"Nancy's information gave me another idea. What if Emily's situation is the same as what happened with Laurie? What if Emily saw something she shouldn't have—something she does not know is important? It could be the reason Hunter and Barnes tried to kill her?"

"I'd say maybe you've got somethin' there, counselor."

23

It was the kind of night Coulter enjoyed. It had been raining all evening, and he'd been entertaining himself by watching the lightning through the glass ceiling of his office. There was a fire in the fireplace, and the only other light came from the candles scattered around the room.

Soc, back to his old self, rubbed against his leg. Coulter reached down to pet him, then opened a beer. Soc demanded his share and Coulter poured a small amount of liquid into his dish. Soc mewed his approval and began lapping it up. It was incredible how spoiled a cat could become.

The front doorbell chimed, sending Soc scurrying across the room in front of Coulter as he went to the front door to open it. A beautiful blond woman wearing a very expensive full-length mink coat stood in the doorway. Coulter noticed a black Mercedes parked in the driveway behind her.

"Mr. McBride?" Her voice was throaty. Coulter wondered if she practiced speaking this way for effect.

"Yep," he replied. "You've got me."

"I'm Marcia Lambert. I understand you will be defending Emily Henderson. Philip Barnes was my brother."

"Yes, I know," he answered. "News sure does travel fast." He held open the door. "Won't you come in?"

Marcia followed him into his office and looked around before settling into a chair.

"Nice room."

"Thanks. Drink?" he asked, turning on several lamps.

"I liked it better without the light. And yes, some white wine would be nice."

She watched as Coulter moved Soc and the saucer of beer out of sight.

"He thinks he owns the place—and he does," Coulter said, smiling. He opened the tiny refrigerator. "I don't have any wine chilled. How about bourbon?"

"I like it straight, no ice." Marcia gave him a forced smile. "May I be candid, Mr. McBride?"

"By all means."

"First, I want to say my marriage is very important to me."

Coulter waited.

"If at all possible, I don't want my husband to know Philip Barnes was my brother."

"Unfortunately, we can't always have what we want."

She eyed him speculatively. "I intend to get exactly what I want. My husband, Buddy, will be a United States Senator. I will go to any lengths to ensure it."

"Perhaps you already have." His voice was cool as he handed her a drink. "Mrs. Lambert, why was your brother blackmailing you?"

Marcia sloshed her drink as she set it down. "How did you find out?"

"You just told me. Rich, politically ambitious husband. Secrets in your past you want to keep hidden. Seedy murder trials don't help much at the polls."

"Philip was such a monster. You have no idea."

"You still haven't answered my question."

"It isn't relevant."

"It is if it gave you a motive to kill your brother."

"Don't be ridiculous. I might have killed Philip, but not both of them." She leaned closer to him. "Keep me out of this mess and I'll make it worth your while."

"No, thanks."

She licked her lips. "I'm not offering just money."

Coulter gave her a cool look. "I know you aren't."

She slipped out of the mink coat. She wore nothing underneath. "Is the answer still no?"

He smiled. "Yes. But thanks anyway."

"I don't mean just ordinary ..."

"Look, why not just tell me what you know? I'm not interested in messing up your life if you're not involved in the murders. My only concern is to save my client's life. If you don't have any relevant information, I won't be bothering you."

"I'll settle for that—for now." She gave him a sultry smile as she slipped back into her coat. "I must tell you I can be very grateful."

Coulter was unmoved. "I'm sure you can."

"Well, you know about Nancy, of course. Philip was also seeing Taylor Niedringhaus. That's Mrs. W. Charles Niedringhaus."

Coulter raised an eyebrow. "As in oil and gas, Mrs. W. Charles Niedringhaus?"

"Uh-huh. The very rich widow. Philip thought he was moving into the big time. He had big plans for Taylor. He was a fool, of course."

"What do you mean?"

"Women like Taylor Niedringhaus can buy all the young studs they want. Philip would have lasted six months, tops."

"How do you know she and your brother weren't in love?"

"Oh, please, spare me. You can't be so naïve."

"Yeah, I guess you're right. Do you know of anyone who might have blown your brother away?"

She shrugged her beautiful shoulders. "Philip made a lot of enemies in his short life. He ran with some very nasty people. Any of them would not have thought twice about taking him out. Of course, he also took a few women to the cleaners. One of them could have done it--you know the old saying about a woman scorned."

"Nancy Osborne mentioned some odd jobs Philip did. Do you happen to know anything about that?"

"No. Wait. Philip came by a few days before his death and demanded money. He said it would be the last time. I figured Taylor Niedringhaus would foot his bills for a while. He stopped by again the next night, drunk and furious. I thought it was strange. Philip rarely showed his emotions, but he could be incredibly nasty. Anyway, he said someone owed him for a job and was refusing to pay."

"Did he mention who the job was for?"

Marcia tossed her blond hair. "No. I made it a practice to know as little about my brother's affairs as possible."

"Why did you come here tonight?" Coulter asked.

"In a high-stakes poker game, it is important to know all the players, don't you think?"

Coulter nodded. "Yeah, I guess you're right."

"I want to know what to expect. Tell me, Mr. McBride, just what should I expect?"

"If you're not involved in any way and I don't need your testimony for any reason, I won't bring you into it, but your name will probably come up. If it were me, I would tell my husband that Philip was my brother, since he's bound to find out, anyway. He probably has more ways to keep the information secret than you do. Your life is not my problem."

"Thanks for being so candid. Maybe it would be better to tell Buddy before anyone else does."

"By the way, Mrs. Lambert, where were you on the morning of September 5th?"

She smiled. "Why, at home with my husband, of course."

Coulter stood up. "Of course. Now, if you will excuse me, I have some lightning to watch."

24

Coulter had been surprised by Ethel Hunter's telephone call asking to meet with him. He was even more surprised that she had wanted to talk about her husband.

Perhaps, he thought as he looked at her, it was guilt. Ethel sat across the desk from him, wearing an ugly red-flowered dress, yet she looked attractive. Her hair was styled, and she was wearing makeup and high-heeled shoes. She no longer wore her former air of defeat.

Ethel Hunter twisted a dainty white handkerchief. "I know I shouldn't speak ill of the dead, Mr. McBride, but life is a lot safer with Jim gone."

"Were you afraid of your husband?"

Ethel nodded her head. "Not for myself. Oh, he slapped me around sometimes, but I could take it. I was so afraid he'd hurt my Cathy. Now I don't have to worry about that anymore."

"Cathy is your daughter?"

"By my previous husband."

"Did Hunter ever threaten her?"

"Not the way you mean. It's just that his hands lingered on her for just a few seconds too long. Sometimes I would catch him looking at her like I'd seen him look at one of our babysitters—the one who won't sit for us anymore."

"I think I understand. Had you planned to leave him?"

Her eyes widened. "Heavens no! Where would I have gone? I couldn't get a decent job—no education. I had to stay. Now there's the pension and the insurance. Mr. McBride, there was $5,000 in a bank account I didn't know Jim had. The passbook was in his locker at the station. I don't have any idea where it came from."

"Maybe your husband was saving a little at a time."

She shook her head. "We never had enough money to go around. Not even with my job. Anyhow, $1,000 was deposited just a week before he died. Doesn't that seem strange?"

"Yes, it does. Did he ever do any extra odd jobs—away from the force?"

"You have to understand, Mr. McBride, my husband was a very secretive man. I didn't dare ask him a lot of questions. Oh, he used to get a lot of strange phone calls. I don't know who from, or what about?"

"Did your husband have any enemies you know of?"

"He could have had. I really don't know of any except Mrs. Henderson. My husband was no good, Mr. McBride, and if that lady killed him, he had it comin'."

She picked at the material in her dress and finally smoothed it down primly over her knees. "What do you think they will do to her?" she asked at last.

"Nothing's going to happen to her if I can help it, except to be set free. She didn't kill your husband, Mrs. Hunter."

Ethel nodded. "Will I have to testify?"

"Maybe. We may need your testimony regarding the money. Or if I find out you know more than you are telling me."

"I've told you everything I know, Mr. McBride, which I realize ain't much. Please don't make me tell about what kind of man my husband was. I know he was bad, but it just wouldn't be right."

"I hope to get at that without having to put you on the stand. I can't promise anything, Mrs. Hunter. Not at this point."

"Well, I guess before it's all over with, everyone's gonna know what kind of man he was. It just can't be helped, can it?"

"No. It can't. By the way, where were you the morning your husband was killed?"

She didn't seem resentful of his question. "I was home with my Cathy." Ethel frowned. "You aren't going to put my little girl on the stand, are you?"

"No. Of course not."

Ethel rose and started toward the door, then turned to face him. "I gotta tell you, Mr. McBride, I didn't kill Jim. But I would have killed him if he had touched my little girl. And I'm glad he's dead. I know that's awful to say, but I can't help it."

"Don't be so hard on yourself. I think your feelings are perfectly natural." He watched her leave. She didn't seem the type to murder anyone—but then, what was the type?

And where did Hunter get the thousand dollars the week before he died?

25

The guard let Emily into Parkland Security's conference room. A few minutes later, an attractive woman, around forty years old, entered the room. She wore an expensive black suit, a lovely white silk blouse, and black high heels.

She smiled at Emily. "I'm guessing from your expression you expected an older gentleman with a tweed jacket, smoking a pipe, and looking at you over bifocals." She held out her hand. "I'm Dr. Hastings-Frost, appointed by the District Attorney, Marshall Lowell."

Emily smiled back as they shook hands.

"I understand you're dealing with mutism. I've brought a couple of notebooks, pens, and my tape recorder. I will take my notes back with me to fill in with the transcription."

"Actually, the mutism left when my husband did. Now I only have problems remembering words I want to say and sometimes stop in the middle of a sentence. Mr. Lowell was very thoughtful in moving me to Parkland. I will try my best to answer any questions you have."

"Okay. May I call you Emily?"

"Sure."

"And I'm Amanda. I've familiarized myself with your file, Emily. I can't begin to know how traumatic the kidnapping must have been for you, and your strength in living through it."

Emily had been apprehensive about meeting with a psychiatrist. Her first impression of Amanda was that she seemed sincere. Coulter had said as long as she told the truth, she had nothing to be afraid of.

"What I am interested in talking about is the Monday night and early Tuesday morning of the murders. I understand you originally planned to spend a few days at Clarice Weitzel's lake house. Let's go back to the time when you returned home to pack. Is this when you picked up your gun?"

"Yes. I started to leave through the den, then decided to take one of my husband's guns with me. I don't remember any particular reason for wanting it at the time."

"Was the gun loaded?"

"No."

"Did you take ammunition?"

"Yes."

"What caliber was the gun?"

".38 caliber."

Amanda made some notes, then turned back to face her. "Emily, can you tell me how you were feeling when you reached the lake house? Were you in pain?"

Emily nodded. "Yes. I was in a great deal of pain from my broken ribs and took my medication after I started a fire in the fireplace."

Amanda looked at her notes. "Those were the pain pills prescribed by Dr. Asher?"

Emily nodded again.

"And I understand you drank some brandy with the pain medication, correct?"

"Yes. I was exhausted, and I finally felt safe enough to fall asleep."

"What time did you wake up?"

"The cold woke me. The fire had burned down, and I'd had a nightmare and was frightened."

"Is that when you loaded the gun?"

"Yes. The nightmare was a horrifying re-run of the assault. I was afraid the men might have followed me. I thought I should protect myself, so I loaded the gun. I had finally realized they had intended to kill me all along. They had tried once. I was afraid they would try again."

Amanda could see the questioning was taking its toll on Emily. "Describe what you did next."

"I put some wood on the burning embers and checked on the time, because I was only supposed to take my pain medication every four hours.

"It was five minutes before ten when I took my pill with a little brandy. It's the last thing I remember until I woke up around nine o'clock Tuesday morning in front of my house. Two officers were waiting to take me into custody."

Amanda chewed on her pencil. "The pain pills and brandy would have lost their effect in four to five hours, just as they did earlier in the evening. You certainly should have awakened by two o'clock Tuesday morning if you had been asleep all that time."

"You don't think I had a drug/alcohol blackout until nine o'clock Tuesday morning?"

Amanda shook her head. "I believe the attempt on your life, together with your physical suffering and trauma, caused post-traumatic stress disorder. The added trauma of your arrest and subsequent meeting with your husband brought on the mutism." Amanda's eyes were compassionate. "If I were asked if you could have committed the murders and not remember, I would have to say it was a possibility. It is crucial to discover your movements between ten p.m. and nine a.m."

"Why do you think I could have committed the murders and not remember doing it?"

"Because post-traumatic stress disorder often triggers situational amnesia."

Emily began rubbing her arms. "Amanda, I am very tired. Could we finish later?"

"Of course. I'll ring for the matron so you can return to your room."

"Thank you."

"I know you're exhausted. Before you go, I would like to clarify the purpose of my meeting with you today. I do not give judgments regarding innocence or guilt. The McNaughton rule relates to whether you were the victim of temporary insanity.

"My assignment is to ascertain whether your defense could be based on the McNaughton rule. I do not give Mr. Lowell my personal opinion, only whether it is a possibility. It is up to a jury to decide whether or not you are guilty."

Amanda pressed the button for the matron. She smiled. "I understand Coulter McBride is representing you. I don't think you could have anyone better."

Emily smiled back at her. "Neither do I." The door opened, and she joined the matron for the trip back to her room.

26

Emily paced the visitors' room as she waited for her meeting with Mary Setting Sun. She hoped Mary could help her open Pandora's box, but feared that if they were successful, unwanted surprises might jump out to bite her.

Her fear of having killed two men was always there, just beneath the surface, but she had reached the point where learning the truth was preferable to not knowing.

· · · · ·

The matron escorted Mary Setting Sun into the room. She wore a denim skirt and jacket, and a bright turquoise blouse which complemented her tawny skin. Black hawk's eyes looked unwaveringly into Emily's. She was surprised to feel herself relax.

Emily had been awake all night, wondering what she would say to this woman. She had finally decided to simply tell the truth, holding nothing back. To do otherwise would defeat her purpose in finding out just what happened on the night of the murders.

When Mary smiled her lovely gold-encased smile, Emily forgot herself. "What happened to your teeth?" she blurted out.

"I fell from a horse when I was very young. You do understand no Indian worth their salt would admit to falling off a horse. Back then, dentists only knew about encasing chipped teeth in gold. He did a good job. The teeth have lasted over fifty years."

"I like them," Emily replied.

"Thank you. I am Coulter's aunt Mary." She sat down and Emily took a chair across from her. "As you know, Mrs. Henderson."

"Please call me Emily," she urged the older woman. "Coulter told me you are a shaman. I know that means you're some kind of medicine woman."

"A shaman is a doctor of the spirit. Someone who helps people to help themselves."

"You mean the shaman doesn't do the healing?"

"A shaman can only point the way. The rest is up to each individual," Mary replied. She took several stones from a drawstring bag and laid them on the table.

"Emily, pick up some stones, one by one, and see if any speak to you."

Emily looked them over and reached for a rough stone of sky blue. She smiled as she held it in her hand. "I feel a calming effect." She looked at it closely. "It's beautiful. What is its name?"

Mary nodded. "Lapis. It is one of my favorites."

Emily reluctantly returned it to the table. A smooth stone of pale pink caught her eye. Her eyes widened as she held it. "I feel a soothing sensation here," she said, "in my stomach."

"For some, rose quartz is very soothing. Your affinity for certain stones tells me much about you. Pick up the bright green one."

Emily picked up the stone. It burned her hand, and she had to drop it.

Mary smiled. "Malachite is not for you. Not yet. There is a warrior within you, Emily. It will take time and effort to awaken her." She put the stones back in their bag and dropped the bag into the pocket of her skirt.

"I don't know whether or not I am guilty of murder," Emily said suddenly. "Could you help me find out? When I try to remember those lost hours, it's like hitting a brick wall."

Mary leaned back in her chair and waited.

Words tumbled from Emily's mouth without her thinking about what she was saying. "After the assault, my mind was out of control. There was so much pressure and a lot of pain. I had terrible thoughts and couldn't stop them. I was so full of anger I thought I'd explode."

"Fear has many faces," Mary said.

Emily fidgeted in her chair, looked slowly around the room, and finally returned her gaze to Mary. "I'm still afraid to sleep because my dreams are, most often, very vivid nightmares."

"Many times, dreams speak to us of things we cannot face when we are awake."

Emily realized she was gripping the arms of the chair and dropped her hands onto her lap. "Why do I keep blaming myself?"

"It is another facet of your fear."

"I have asked myself over and over again—why me?" Emily dropped her head.

"Did you and your husband discuss what happened to you?"

"I tried. He refused to listen to me. Refused to believe me. He seemed more frustrated and angry with me than anything. Then, when I was arrested, Dan's mind was already made up. He was sure I was guilty."

"His betrayal must have caused you great sorrow."

"I've never felt such sadness as when I saw what was in his eyes," Emily replied.

"You must put these feelings in the past where they belong. You will begin to heal when you learn to trust in yourself."

Emily stood up and began to pace. "When the pain gets too bad, I've learned to shut off all feeling."

Mary's eyes bored into Emily's. "And you have learned that does not work. You have no choice. You must look inside yourself and face what you find there. If you do, the pain will disappear."

Emily turned suddenly toward the older woman and blurted. "I don't feel alive. Hunter and Barnes killed me—they just didn't bury my body. Even Dan will tell you his wife is gone forever. And he's right!"

Mary said nothing as Emily paced in front of her. Suddenly Emily sat down, her anger dissipated. "I'm glad the wimp who was Emily Henderson no longer exists."

Mary's eyes snapped. "The wimp isn't completely gone. It is time you stopped feeling sorry for yourself. You are not dead. You must look inside yourself."

Emily leaned back in her chair and closed her eyes. Five minutes went by, then ten. She forgot Mary was in the room. She sighed and began to remember out loud.

"From the very beginning, that Friday was different. I was thinking of my mother in the morning. I haven't thought of her in a very long time."

Mary remained quiet.

"The memory was like a picture in my mind. I was five years old, and I was lying in bed watching her get ready to go out."

Emily opened her eyes and glanced at Mary. The old woman seemed to be asleep.

"Mama had on this beautiful red dress and high-heeled shoes with ankle straps. She pulled up her dress to adjust her garter belt, and she was laughing and teasing me. Mama was so much fun."

"Where was your father?" Mary asked.

Emily frowned. "I never knew who my father was." After a moment, she closed her eyes and continued. "Grandma came in. She was very angry with mama. She said mama was a sinner who danced and drank and would go to hell."

"What did your mother say?"

"She just laughed and kissed me goodnight, and then she left."

"What else do you remember about this time?"

Emily closed her eyes and shook her head as if she couldn't bear to think about it. "I woke up because someone was banging on the front door. I crept to the stairs and looked down. Grandma was down below talking to a policeman. I heard him tell her that mama was dead." Emily's voice broke.

Mary waited until Emily had regained her composure. "You miss your mother a great deal," Mary whispered.

Emily nodded. "And I had to hide it. Grandma said I must never be like her."

"Maybe your grandmother was grieving in her own way."

"No! Grandma never loved her," Emily protested. "She kept telling me that mama was bad."

"Emily," Mary spoke quietly, "It is important for you to understand why your thoughts were so much with your mother that day. A part of you knew your trial-by-fire was coming. Your mother wanted you to remember how much she loves you and still watches over you."

"My heart was filled with longing for my mother. During my lunch hour, I bought a garter belt and a pair of stockings, and when I came back, I put them on."

"Did wearing them make you feel close to your mother?"

"Yes. I felt free, as she must have. I wore them to the company dinner."

"Just like your mother would have done."

Emily paced in front of Mary and finally spoke without looking at her. "When I fell into the river, the stockings and garter belt were destroyed. A part of me is afraid I am like mama."

"There is also a part of you that knows your mother was not bad at all."

"Yes. How did you know?"

"So, we have the woman you believe you should be—the woman you fear you might be—and the woman who is capable of just being. All three want to be you. So, what are you to do about these three parts of Emily?"

"I have no idea," Emily said, laughing.

Mary stared into Emily's eyes and nodded. "Laughter is a good start."

"I loved my mother more than anybody and grandma couldn't stand it. I wasn't allowed to dance or have a real boyfriend until Dan came along. She encouraged me to date him. He had recently moved to Abilene and became very active in our church. Actually, now when I think about it, my grandmother and Dan are very much alike."

Mary sighed. "Your mother died because she was bad, and you were hurt because you were bad. Is this what the voice inside you whispers?"

"Yes."

Mary spoke softly as she touched Emily's cheek. "You have kept so many feelings buried until now. Your trial-by-fire is bringing them out of hiding and you will be forced to deal with them."

"Why did all of this happen to me?"

"You chose this path a long time ago. I have been asked to help you. There is nothing you can do to stop the wheel from turning, Emily. You are being tested, and you will be tested much more before the iron of your will is forged."

Oddly, Emily wasn't afraid. On some level, she understood.

Mary reached into her shoulder bag. "We have much work to do. I have brought some books which may help you." She handed Emily a book with an old Indian woman on the cover.

"This is a book about another woman's trials by fire. Your journey also will not be easy, but there is a reason, and eventually it will become clear to you. You must decide if you want to walk this path, wherever it leads. There is not much time before your will is tested again."

"*Promises to keep, and miles to go before I sleep.* I wonder why that popped into my head?" Emily mused. "Somehow, I know I don't have a choice. I want and need your help, Mary. I am so grateful you are here to guide me."

Mary nodded. "We have walked the path together before, you and I. You made promises before you came into this life. I am pleased you have decided to keep them." She handed Emily another book.

"These are yoga exercises which will help you become physically strong. The first thing you must learn is how to breathe." Mary sat on the floor, crossed her legs, and rested her hands on her knees.

"I can tell from the way you breathe, your ribs are causing you pain."

"Yes, but I won't take any more drugs."

Mary nodded. "You need to know the truth of how your body is healing. Do this exercise as often as you can. Breathe in through your nose, hold, and breathe out through your mouth. But concentrate on your stomach."

Emily joined her on the floor. After several tries, she smiled. "Yes, I can feel it."

"Now I'll show you how some other postures are done. Yoga is the perfect exercise. You need very little room and nothing except yourself."

They worked together a while longer, but eventually Mary rose and put on her moccasins. She picked up another book and handed it to Emily. "I will return in a few days and we will talk again."

Emily's eyes widened as she took the well-worn paperback and glanced at the title.

Mary smiled. "You were expecting only Native American philosophy?"

Emily reddened. "I guess so."

"There are many great teachers. This book will tell you more about 'promises to keep'."

Emily took Mary's hands in hers. "I have never spoken of it to anyone, but I know you were with me that Friday night. I saw and heard you in my mind. You gave me the courage to save my life."

"You are wrong. I could not give you courage. I only reminded you of it."

Emily looked into Mary's beautiful eyes. "You know why this is happening to me, don't you?"

"It is time you took back your personal power. It was taken from you a long time ago. You must become a spiritual warrior again. And as we just discussed, you have promises to keep."

. . . .

Emily laid on her bunk thinking about her afternoon with Mary. She was no longer afraid of what the future would bring. "There is a warrior within you," Mary had said. She picked up one book and began to read.

27

As Coulter headed for the Tumble Inn, he wondered what Wanda Sikorsky had going for her that caused Dan Henderson to cheat on his wife.

When he arrived, it was almost closing time. Coulter found a stool at a bar that looked exactly like a thousand other shit-kickin' Texas honkey tonks. Waylon was wailing from the jukebox. There was the smell of stale beer and cigarette butts. The lights were turned low, so the people—as well as the whole joint—looked their best.

It was a rude shock to the die-hards when the lights came up at closing time.

Coulter was told Wanda was the manager and usually tended bar. The description they had given him was good, and he spotted her at the other end of the room.

She was playing liars' poker and leaning against the back-bar. One leg was cocked up, revealing a smooth tanned flank under her shorts. Her chest was thrust out, giving the guys a good look at what was beneath the sleeveless tank top. Coulter admitted to himself it was a pleasant view.

Wanda's eyes cut to Coulter, then back to the bill in her hand. The guy she was playing with must have called. She smiled and handed him her bill.

The man swore, and she laughed as she grabbed both bills and came toward Coulter.

Wanda Sikorsky was tiny, not much over five feet tall. He guessed her to be around thirty years old. She might be older. The dim lighting hid a lot of flaws. One thing was obvious. She didn't spend all of her time in a bar. A body like hers only came from working out constantly.

Dan must have a thing for small women. It probably made him feel like a big man—though he wasn't over five feet nine.

Wanda strutted toward Coulter with a fast twist, her hips gyrating. Even at a distance, she gave off an aura of pure animal sexuality. She enjoyed her effect on the men watching her and sent out a signal saying she could and would unleash that animal sexuality only if it struck her fancy.

Her black hair was thick and cut in a shoulder-length pageboy with choirboy bangs. She posed in front of him, smiling, revealing tiny white teeth and deep dimples in both cheeks. As she leaned forward, Coulter could see her eyes, and it wiped away any appearance of innocence. Her eyes were green stones, cold and hard.

She gave Coulter a slow once-over and apparently liked what she saw. Her smile now was intimate, as if they shared a secret.

"So what'll it be, Ace?"

"Stolie on the rocks, please." He laid a twenty on the bar. Yeah, Wanda was the kind of woman who Dan, and a lot of men before and after him, would find impossible to leave alone.

"My kind of guy," she drawled. "You didn't have the look of a beer drinker."

She expertly free-poured his drink over ice.

"Would you join me?" Coulter asked before she had a chance to move back to the other end of the bar.

"Sure. Why not?" She poured herself a double shot and sipped it slowly while studying him over the rim of her glass. "You don't belong in a place like this. What are you doing here? Slumming?"

Coulter ignored her comment. "I heard a guy down the way call you Wanda. Would you be Wanda Sikorsky?"

Her smile lingered. Her eyes turned to flint. "You a cop? Nah, you're not a cop. Do I know you?"

Coulter shook his head. "Not yet. The name's Coulter."

"You got a last name?"

He hesitated a second before answering. "McBride."

She laughed. "I knew who you were. I was just messing with you. I saw your picture in the paper. You're the cop killer's lawyer."

"Alleged cop killer."

"Whatever. I guess you're here to size up old Dan's paramour. Right?"

Coulter smiled. "Something like that. I was told recently it's a good idea to meet the entire cast of players."

"Dan and I had a thing going for a while. Nothing long-term. I don't go in for long-term. He knows how to show a girl a good time. Not much in the brains department. I like that in a guy." She smiled knowingly. "Now you? You're dangerous. In case I forgot to mention it, I am especially fond of dangerous."

Coulter smiled back. "I'd say you are the one who is dangerous. Just for the record, was Dan Henderson with you the night of the killings?"

"Uh, huh. We had a little party after the bar closed. There were four of us here."

"Mind telling me who they were?"

"Well, there was Dan, me, and Tiffany. She's one of our waitresses— and Max something or other. Max came in real late. He took a shine to Tiffany. Of course, he was drunk. He spent money like it was water. After we closed, we just kept on partying."

"Is Tiffany around?"

"It's her night off. She'll be here the rest of the week. You can stop by again if you want."

"I don't suppose you'd give me her phone number."

Wanda smiled, giving him the full dimple effect again. "Now you know better than that. If I give you her number, you might not come back to see me."

Coulter shrugged. "Well, thanks anyway. I'll stop by again."

Wanda ran her hands down her hips. "I'll be here, sugar."

Coulter saw her glance up and quickly look away as a young girl emerged from the lady's room and stepped behind the service bar.

"Who is she?" Coulter nodded toward the young girl.

"Guess I forgot Tiffany was still here. She was helping out earlier. I'll send her over and give you a chance to talk."

Wanda moved back to the other end of the bar, spoke to Tiffany, and recommended her game of liars' poker.

Coulter carried his drink to a table as Tiffany came toward him.

"Hi, I'm Tiffany. Wanda said you wanted to talk to me."

"Right. I'm Coulter McBride." He got up and held out a chair. She looked surprised, then smiled as she sat down. He took the chair across the table.

Coulter wondered what the hell this kid was doing here. She was too young to be working in a bar. Tiffany had a sweet, guileless face and an Oklahoma twang.

"So, where are you from, Tiffany?" Coulter asked.

"I grew up in Durant, Oklahoma." She grinned. "My real name is Gladys Faye. Ain't that awful? I changed it to Tiffany as soon as I left town.

"When was that?"

"About six months ago. I was lucky to land a job here. I graduated high school, then couldn't find a job back home. Or anywhere else 'till I got here."

Tiffany was talking a mile a minute, so Coulter decided not to interrupt.

"I get asked a lot why I'm working in a place like this. A girl's gotta eat. I already found out about good Christians the hard way." She laughed. "I decided to see what wicked sinners were like. Want to know the difference? The guys who come in here don't pretend they're something they're not. I hate phonies and liars, Mr. McBride." She blushed. "Sorry, I got carried away. I do sometimes."

"I wanted to ask you about the night or morning the two cops were murdered."

"Wanda said you wanted to ask me about that. Wanda and me had a party after hours the mornin' the policemen were killed. I remember 'cause everybody was talking about it the next night."

"How late were you here at the bar?" Coulter asked.

"Till about six o'clock. Me and Max went out to Denny's for breakfast," she paused, blushing. "Wanda was still asleep. Dan got real drunk and was passed out for a while. He woke up and left about five o'clock."

"I don't know if Wanda told you. I'm Emily Henderson's lawyer."

"The woman who killed the two policemen?"

Coulter smiled. "The woman I'm trying to prove didn't kill the two policemen."

"No, she didn't say anything about you," Tiffany replied.

"Dan is Emily's husband."

Tiffany's eyes were as wide as saucers. "Really? Oh, my gosh."

"Yeah. So tell me, what do you think of Wanda?"

Tiffany looked uncomfortable. "She's been good to me, gave me this job."

"What is she like?"

Tiffany leaned forward and lowered her voice. "To tell you the truth, Mr. McBride, I'm kind of scared of her."

"Why, if you don't mind my asking?"

"Well, she's got this temper. I mean, one minute she can be jokin' and laughin' and then," Tiffany snapped her fingers, "she turns all mean. I'm sayin' real mean." She glanced at the bar, saw Wanda watching her, and quickly stood up. "I better go."

Coulter didn't press her to finish. He didn't want her to get into trouble. Besides, he had most of the information he had come for.

He laid twenty dollars on the table and stood up. "Thanks for your time, Tiffany. It's a very pretty name, by the way."

She smiled. "You're a real nice man. I hope I helped you."

"You did." He hesitated. "If you ever decide to look for a different job, I'd like to return the favor. No strings attached," he added, catching the look on her face. "A friend of mine is head of the Women's Crisis Center. She has a lot of contacts. You could stay there until you got on your feet. Anyway, here's my card, just in case."

Tiffany glanced back toward the bar. Wanda had turned the other way. She quickly took the card and slipped it into her jeans pocket before walking away.

• • • • • •

Coulter and Soc had just settled into bed when the phone rang.

"Mr. McBride, it's Tiffany from the bar."

"Yeah, Tiffany. What's wrong?"

"Wanda gave me the third degree after the bar closed. I must have said somethin' wrong. She got real mad. I'm scared, Mr. McBride."

"Where are you? I'll pick you up."

"I'm at the Center Motel, down the street from the bar. I'll be watching for you."

"It will take me about twenty minutes." Coulter threw on his clothes and grabbed his cell phone as he hurried to his car.

When he pulled into the motel, Tiffany ran toward him carrying a small suitcase. He opened the door for her and put her suitcase in the back. Anger flooded him when he saw her face. Her lip was cut, and she'd have a black eye from the bruise on her cheekbone.

"I'm sorry to bother you. I didn't know what else to do," she cried.

"Hush. I called the Women's Center. My friend Clarice is expecting you."

28

Mary Setting Sun was escorted into the Parkland visitors' room the next afternoon. She smiled at Emily as she sat down and slipped off her moccasins. "Ah, much better." She studied Emily. "I am sorry you are having a difficult day."

"I panic when I think about the trial. I may spend the rest of my life in prison, or even receive the death penalty. Yoga and studying the books you gave me help get my mind off it up to a point. But Coulter's working so hard while I'm doing nothing."

"You have been forced to spend much time alone. There is another week before your trial begins. Try to meditate as much as possible. It will help free you from your mind's prison cell."

Emily's arms were red where she had been rubbing them. "I try so hard to remember what happened that Monday night. I'm no closer than when I started."

"The mind cannot be forced. You were being tested when you faced death. You fought back and won. The trial is not the next test of your will, Emily, for there will be no trial. This is also Coulter's trial-by-fire."

Emily's eyes widened. "No trial? How do you know?"

"I was told by the Snake Kingdom. It was a member of the Snake Kingdom who asked for my help before Coulter did, and why I was with you that morning."

Emily laughed. "I'm not sure I want to hear about the Snake Kingdom just now."

"I think it would be good for you to know. Do you remember when you were ten years old, and you were eating apples under the tree and a snake was with you? You were talking to it. When your grandmother saw the two of you, she came running with a hoe in her hands. You told the snake it must run away before it was killed.

"Then last year at Christmas time you had been shopping, and you went to bed and left all your packages on the floor. The next morning, there was a snake on top of the packages. You told it to leave. It told you it wanted to stay with you while your husband was away.

"You let it lie on the bed next to you and it stayed until your husband was due back. You explained it needed to leave before your husband saw it."

Emily stared at her for several minutes. "How in the world could you know all of that?"

"I just told you, the Snake Kingdom gave me the information. Now, let's get back to the present. You must clear your mind. First, forgive yourself, then forgive everyone else. It will be difficult. The most important task for you is to forgive the two men who harmed you."

"No! I can't do it." she cried.

Mary smoothed back Emily's hair. "Then you will never be free of them. They will always hide in the dark corners of your mind."

"I can't stand to hear any more!"

"Emily, you must stop being a victim. Let the festering wounds inside you heal."

"I want to leave now." Emily jumped up and rang for the matron.

"You can't run away from yourself," Mary said softly.

Emily's shoulders sagged as she turned to face Mary. "I've found that out."

"When I say forgive, I mean to release them from your mind. Accept what happened and move on. I should have said let go instead of forgive. You are holding your mind hostage. It must be free to remember, as well as look to the future." Mary slipped on her moccasins and stood up.

Emily gave her a small smile. "Letting go sounds easier than forgiving. I know—more meditation."

"Your imagination can carry you away beyond these walls into a world of your own making. I would like you to use your energy to practice smelling, touching, and tasting. I think this will help you."

"What should I do?"

"Practice imagining how these things feel: A horse's muzzle, the petal of a rose and the thorn, the sun on your face, walking in a warm drizzle, the crunch of snow underfoot, the foam of beer on your lip, walking barefoot on gravel, and creek mud between your toes.

"Visualize the smell of smoke from a log cabin, new cut grass, a summer carnival, early summer lilac. Visualize the taste of a lemon, crunchy fried catfish, a hamburger with onions and pickles. And lastly, hear your favorite song.

"These are excellent exercises for your mind. Here, I have written them down." Mary handed Emily the paper, then hugged her. "You can do this!"

Emily smiled as the door opened. "I'll do my best."

"It will be enough. You and Coulter are karmically tied. Together you may emerge reborn after your trials-by-fire. Strange as it may seem, you both should be grateful for this opportunity."

29

"I just put a rhubarb pie in the oven." The soft East Texas drawl on the other end of the phone couldn't belong to anyone except Marshall Lowell. Coulter smiled as he waited for what seemed five minutes for the District Attorney to get the last few words out.

"If this is an invitation, I'll be there in fifteen minutes."

"Make it twenty. The chicken-fried steaks will be ready by then." The phone went dead.

Coulter's mouth watered in anticipation as he wondered why Lowell had invited him to dinner. To hell with it. He'd find out soon enough. He changed from suit and tie to tee-shirt and jeans. This would not be a suit and tie evening.

Lowell had grown up in an orphanage in Marshall, Texas, the source of his first name. He'd worked his way through college and law school—where he was number one in his class.

He was hand-picked to be the law clerk of the brilliant Federal Court Judge, Martin Spencer, now a Justice on the Texas Supreme Court. Lowell's record as District Attorney was a legend, as was his East Texas drawl. He spoke so slowly, opposing attorneys were hard-pressed not to finish his sentences for him.

Roses of every color bloomed in the flowerbeds along the driveway of 2322 Monticello. Coulter rang the bell as he looked inside through the stained-glass portion of the new front door. A crystal chandelier, also new, gleamed in the entrance hall.

Marshall Lowell, chef's apron tied around his more than ample waist, smiled as he opened the door. "Right on time."

"What've you done to the place?"

"Harriet had the whole dang thing remodeled. Except for the kitchen, of course. Ain't nobody except me touching my kitchen."

Coulter handed him a twelve-pack of Lone Star Longnecks, Lowell's favorite beverage after sweet ice tea. They moved through the house into Lowell's exclusive territory. It was quite a kitchen. Sage, chives, and other herbs which Coulter couldn't identify grew in plant boxes resting in the huge window above the double sink. A top-of-the-line Jenn Aire Range with grill was also new.

Lowell popped the caps on two longnecks, handed one to Coulter, and put the rest into the industrial size refrigerator. Coulter sat down at a round oak table full of nicks and cigarette burns—no doubt acquired during Lowell's monthly poker-and-chili nights.

Lowell drank half of his beer in one long swallow as he moved to the large island in the middle of the room. Grease sizzled in a well-seasoned iron skillet around two huge chicken-fried steaks. "Almost done," he said.

Coulter admired the framed newspaper clippings extolling Lowell's prowess as a chili chef supreme. He had won the local chili cook-off so many times they retired him from competition and he was now a judge.

Lowell was famous not only as a prosecutor but also as one of the finest country cooks in the Southwest. His chicken-fried steak was orgasmic. Mashed potatoes, cream gravy, and biscuits were already on the table, along with black-eyed peas, collard greens, and a side platter filled with jalapenos, freshly sliced tomatoes, and green onions.

Coulter gave the gravy the spoon test. It passed, as he knew it would. The spoon stood proudly upright in the thick gravy.

"Pour us some tea," Lowell said.

Coulter reached for the pitcher and ice bucket. "I assume this is sweet tea."

Lowell grinned. "Is there any other kind?" He removed the chicken-fried steaks to the waiting plates, setting one in front of Coulter and the other in front of his place.

There was complete silence as they filled their plates and began their feast, both men concentrating on their food.

Coulter leaned back when he'd cleaned his plate and considered loosening the belt on his jeans. Lowell finished a few minutes later. He removed their plates, took the rhubarb pie out of the oven to cool, and poured two cups of coffee.

Lowell sighed. "My favorite meal and I can only have it when Harriet leaves town. She swears it goes directly into my arteries."

Coulter smiled. "It's worth it. By the way, I had some of your chili and cornbread a few days ago. You haven't lost your touch."

Lowell smiled his thanks.

"Why don't you quit the law and open a restaurant, become filthy rich, and make us defense attorneys happy?"

"I'd miss a good fight, like the one we've got coming up."

Coulter and his father belonged to an elite group of criminal defense attorneys who had the distinction of winning a court case that Lowell had personally tried. Their number could be counted on one hand.

"Okay," Coulter continued, "You know how curious I am. There must be a hundred guys who'd kill for the chance to join you for this superb feast. How'd you happen to choose me?"

"I enjoy your company. It gives me a lot of satisfaction to cook a meal and watch a man appreciate my food as much as I do. Besides, I told Bannister I'd like to give you the news. We got DNA matches in the Laurie Weitzel case. They're a match for Hunter and Barnes, so we can put that one to bed. I also wanted to kick around the Henderson case a little."

"Did Bannister fill you in on my conversation with Nancy Osborne?"

"Yeah. I assume she is on your list of suspects," Lowell replied.

"You assume correctly. The list is getting quite long."

Lowell sipped his coffee. "Interesting case. Gives our police force a black eye. Dr. Hastings-Frost says your client's a nice girl with post-traumatic stress disorder. She also says Emily could have murdered the two guys and not remember doing it. Poor memory won't get her off the hook."

Coulter waited.

"Since you know about the Laurie Weitzel tie-in, I figure you might go for the 'needed killin' defense. Sorry, that dog won't hunt."

"I'm staying with 'not guilty.' She didn't do it, Lowell."

"What have you got as a defense, Coulter? Nothing. You'll lose, my friend. Hunter and Barnes were real bad boys, which will give her points with the jury, though not enough. I've been getting some calls. Dragging out our dirty laundry is not a good idea. This is all off the record, of course."

"Of course."

"The State says capital murder is a mandatory death penalty case. As I said, there's been some conversation. The consensus is it will save the taxpayers a lot of money, and it will save you and me a lot of midnight oil, if we reach an agreement before the case comes to trial."

"What kind of agreement?"

"If Emily Henderson pleads guilty now, she gets life in prison without the possibility of parole. If she doesn't, we go to the mat. With her confession, the evidence we have, along with motive and opportunity, your client heads to death row. What Emily has to decide is whether to roll the dice."

Coulter finished his coffee. "You think the pie has cooled down enough?"

"Only one way to find out." Lowell brought the pie to the table on its trivet, cut two enormous slices, and dished them up as Coulter poured more coffee. Silence prevailed until both plates were clean.

"Ecstasy. The rhubarb has the perfect amount of tartness. Though I hate to use a cliché, the crust is so flaky it melts in your mouth." Coulter sighed and poured them another cup of coffee.

"The cops grilled her for hours until they got a confession," Coulter said. "You know I'll get it thrown out. All you have is circumstantial evidence, and not very good evidence at that."

"There's a lot of it. Granted, we have no eyewitness. We do have strong motives and opportunity. Your client's mind is messed up, she has no alibi, and last but not least, she threatened to kill them—more than once. Frankly, I wouldn't blame her."

"Neither would I."

Lowell frowned. "You really think she's innocent?"

"Yep."

"I think she is guilty as hell, but I don't think she deserves to be executed." Lowell picked up their plates and placed them in the sink. "By the way, in case you don't already know, three long-distance phone calls were made from Clarice's lake house. The first one was to the Women's Crisis Center around five in the afternoon on the 4th. The second was to information at 1:05 a.m. on the 5th. The third, at 1:58 a.m., was to the 523rd Precinct. The desk sergeant remembered a woman asking for Barnes, which apparently wasn't too unusual because he said another woman called for Barnes around 2:00 a.m. Both women were told Barnes was out on patrol."

Coulter felt like someone had kicked him in the stomach. One good thing about Lowell talking so slowly, it gave him time to compose himself. If the jury thought Emily was guilty of premeditated murder, there was no chance of acquittal. Those phone calls were a bombshell that had just exploded in his face.

"I'll pass your offer on to Mrs. Henderson. It's her life and her call. You were right when you said Hunter and Barnes were bad boys. My investigation's dug up more than one woman who wanted them dead. I just haven't figured out who got there first."

"She's got a week. Keep me up to date on discovery and I'll do the same," Lowell said.

Coulter stood up to go. Lowell followed him to the door.

"Thanks for dinner. Never had better," Coulter said.

Lowell flipped on the porch light. "Good to see you back in harness. I do love a worthy adversary."

30

Coulter drove home from Lowell's on automatic pilot. He walked into his office without turning on the lights and stared through the glass wall at the shimmering path the full moon made across the lake.

Lowell was right. Coulter had no real defense, just a lot of loose threads. He dreaded the next morning when he had to tell Emily about Lowell's offer. With less than a week until trial, she'd have to make her decision. If she asked for his opinion, he didn't know what he'd answer.

The telephone calls from the lake house made a huge difference. They were incriminating, yet there was a chance they might trigger Emily's memory. He wouldn't bet on it, though. Difficult as it was, he had to face the possibility that it was Emily who made those calls. And why she had made them.

Surely Clarice had received her phone bill for the lake house. Why hadn't she told him about the long-distance calls? He glanced at his watch. It was only nine o'clock. He picked up the phone and called the Center. Tiffany answered the phone.

"Mr. McBride, hi. I called you. No one was home. I didn't leave a message."

"How are you doing? And call me Coulter."

"Just great, Coulter. Clarice is helping me find a job. In the meantime, I'm doing odd jobs here around the Center. I love answering the phones and I'm used to working nights."

"Is Clarice there, Tiffany?"

"Yes, sir, she is. You want to talk to her?"

"Please." He heard Tiffany call out, and Clarice came on the line.

"Hey there, stranger," she said. "How's it going?"

"Not so great. Will you be there for a while, or are you headed home?"

"I'll probably be here until midnight. Got a lot of paperwork to catch up on."

"Would it be okay if I stop by? I'd like to talk to you about a couple of things."

"I'll put on a fresh pot of coffee."

• • • •

Tiffany saw Coulter at the door and rushed to open it. "Hi, Mr. McBride— I mean Coulter. Clarice's waiting for you in her office. After you finish talking, I have something to tell you. I'll be here answering the phones."

"Okay. I'll see you later."

Clarice was muttering under her breath and working on a pile of papers when Coulter walked into her office. "Those wouldn't be cuss words you're saying under your breath, would they?"

Clarice laughed. "Guilty. How about a cup of coffee?"

"Great."

He settled down in a chair across from her desk. "First of all, I heard the news about the DNA in Laurie's case. After all this time, at last you know what happened."

Clarice's eyes filled with tears. "I've finally found some peace. I only wish the bastards could have been killed more than once. I hope the first shot was to their groins."

"I just had what many would consider—including me—the most delicious meal ever. Lowell invited me to dinner. Chicken fried steak and all the trimmings, and rhubarb pie."

Clarice smiled. "You have indeed been blessed. How is the old cuss, anyway?"

"Tricky as ever. He wanted to talk about Emily's case."

"Did he have any new information?" Clarice asked.

"He dropped a bomb on me. Three calls were made from your lake house. One was to the Center when Emily arrived. Another was made to information at 1:05 a.m. and a third at 1:58 to the 523rd precinct. They know the callers were women, and, yes, they were told Barnes was on patrol. Also, the desk clerk said another woman had called for Barnes."

"Oh, oh!"

"Clarice, did you get a copy of the phone bill for the lake house?"

Her face turned red. "You are wondering why I didn't tell you about the calls. The answer is, I didn't know about any calls." She motioned to the pile of papers on her desk. "I have automatic payment for all my utilities through my bank account. Most times, I don't open the bills for weeks."

"I pay mine the same way. The thing is, Clarice, the trial is less than a week away and I don't have a defense. Lowell didn't have anything to hang his hat on until those phone call records. You know he'll be pushing premeditated."

"Yeah. If only Emily could get her memory back. She might have an alibi. What are you going to do?"

"The only thing I can do," Coulter replied. "Keep on digging and pray for a miracle. By the way, I never got around to asking where you were that night, or I should say morning."

"I was home. Sleeping for a change until Bannister called to tell me what happened. Am I a suspect?"

"A case could be made that you were the only other person who could have made those phone calls, and you did get rid of Emily's gun."

"Coulter, I didn't..."

He held up his hand, palm out. "Stop. I don't think you killed anybody. I just wanted to clear the air between us because I figure—you figured—I thought you might have."

"You know," Clarice said, "it wasn't a woman, and it might not mean anything—Dan telephoned me earlier in the evening. He had found

Emily's note saying she was staying with a friend. He asked if she was with me, and I said she was at my lake house on Grapevine Lake. He asked for her phone number and I gave it to him. I can't imagine it is anything."

Coulter ran his hand through his hair. "No, neither can I."

He poured himself another cup of coffee. "How is Tiffany getting along?"

"She's a sweet kid. We'll find her a job in no time. She told me how you helped her."

"Yeah, well, my motive is partly selfish. I still have Dan and Wanda Sikorsky, Tiffany's boss, high on my list of suspects. As a matter of fact, Tiffany wants to talk with me before I leave." He stood up to go.

Clarice walked with him to the door and squeezed his hand. "If there is anything I can do, just ask."

He leaned down and kissed her on the cheek. "I appreciate you letting Tiffany stay at the Center."

31

Tiffany was still busy answering the phones. Coulter sat down to wait.

"I think I'd like a job as a receptionist," she said. "I love talking on the phone."

"You would be great at it. Now, what would you like to talk to me about?"

She looked around as if someone might overhear them and lowered her voice. "Maybe I know something that might help you. You've been so good to me. I love it here at the Center. Thank you for bringing me here. I'm still afraid Wanda will find me."

"There is something I need to tell you. I saw the two policemen's pictures on the TV. Do you remember the night I met you when I started to tell you about Wanda being so mad?"

"Yeah, I remember."

"Well, the man she was so mad at was one of the policemen–– the young one. She was mad at him something awful. He was there at the bar a couple of nights before he was killed."

Coulter sat upright in his chair and grabbed a pen and notebook from his pocket. "The young policeman's name was Barnes. This is a real break, Tiffany."

"I'm just glad to be able to help." The phone rang. "I'll be right back."

Coulter waited while Tiffany answered another call. Though he was impatient, he didn't want to rush her. His gut told him what she had to say could be the break he was waiting for.

"Sorry I took so long," Tiffany said. "I didn't tell you everything about the night of the murders. There was somethin' even before then."

"It's okay, just take your time."

"Dan started coming into the bar right after I went to work there. Anybody could see he was crazy about Wanda. She went out with him a couple of times. I could tell she was gettin' tired of him. Then all of a sudden she started acting real crazy about him."

"Maybe she fell for him," Coulter said.

"At first I thought so, too. One night she got drunk and bragged about how men were stupid, and how easy it was to control 'em. I asked her if she was gonna marry Dan. She laughed and said, 'You gotta be kidding, but the jerk may come into some money and I sure could use me some.'

"Anyway, one night the young policeman—Barnes—came in after the bar was closed and everyone else had gone. They sat and drank together. She didn't act like he was a boyfriend or anything. It looked like she was real serious."

"Did you hear anything they said?"

"No. I was cleanin' up at the other end of the bar."

"Tiffany, do you know if Barnes and Dan Henderson ever met?"

"I'm pretty sure they didn't. The policeman was only there one other time. That's when she got so mad at him. She didn't know I saw them. She thought I'd already gone home. After he left, Wanda was still furious. I'd never seen her like that, mean like a snake, then kind of quiet like she was tryin' to figure something out."

"This is important, Tiffany. What about the morning of the murders? The night you had the party with Dan and Wanda."

"I was comin' to that."

Coulter held his breath.

"I didn't tell a lie, Coulter. They were at the bar, and the four of us did party. Dan Henderson was dead drunk, like I said, and Wanda took him to the back storeroom. There's a sofa back there. Dan left about five o'clock.

"The thing is, I didn't see Wanda after about one-thirty in the morning. Me and Max decided to go for breakfast around six. I went to the storeroom to see if Wanda wanted to go with us. She was gone. I lied to you about Wanda being there because I was scared of her. There's a back door out of the storeroom. She must have gone out that way. I don't have any idea what time she left.

"It's okay, Tiffany. You wouldn't have any way of knowing the connection."

"I should've known somethin' was wrong. When you came in the other night, she said if you asked, I was to say she was there until six o'clock."

Coulter smiled as he got up to leave. "Don't worry about it. I'm just glad you told me now."

As Coulter started for home, he wondered how in the hell he would go about flushing out Wanda.

32

Coulter waited in front of the black-lacquered double door of Taylor Niedringhaus's penthouse apartment. Her secretary had called to advise Coulter she had returned to the City. He wasn't sure if he needed to talk with her. Still, she might know something of value.

While waiting, he reminded himself of her past. Taylor's mother had died when Taylor was about eight years old. Her father started an oil drilling supply company and parlayed it into wildcat oil strikes, making theirs one of the richest companies in the State. Taylor worked with her dad in the oil fields every step of the way. Upon her father's death, she became head of Taylor Oil and Gas.

She'd fallen fell in love with, and married, W. Charles Niedringhaus. She was rich enough that his blue-blooded but poor family didn't object to her lack of pedigree.

Then early one Saturday morning, Taylor got a phone call while she and W. Charles were still in bed. The caller, the former husband of W. Charles' secretary, thought Taylor would like to know the reason for his divorce was the discovery of his wife's year-long affair with W. Charles. Taylor kicked W. Charles' blue-blooded butt out of her bed, and her life.

She was reputed to be intelligent and street-smart, which Coulter considered an unbeatable combination. He looked forward to meeting her.

Taylor Niedringhaus answered the door herself. She wore a denim shirt, jeans, and black lizard cowboy boots. She was almost as tall as Coulter. Though she had to be around fifty years old, Coulter thought she looked damned good in her jeans.

Taylor held out a tanned hand. Her grip was firm and her smile genuine. "Nice to meet you, Mr. McBride. Come on in."

Coulter followed her into a living room, which afforded an incredible view of the city far below. "Thank you for seeing me, Mrs. Niedringhaus."

"Call me Taylor." She motioned him to the bar. "How about a drink? No reason we can't relax while we chat. Bourbon on the rocks okay?"

"Bourbon's fine. And it's Coulter." He glanced around a room filled with Asian antiques. A magnificent jade lion over the mantel of the fireplace caught his eye.

Taylor followed his gaze. "My ex-husband found it in Singapore on one of his many trips abroad." He noticed her tone was just a tad sarcastic.

"It's a beautiful piece," Coulter replied.

"I prefer the Remingtons at my ranch. W.C. decorated this place, and I never bothered to change it. I just stay here when I come into town." She handed him a Texas-sized bourbon on the rocks and took one for herself.

"Taylor, I'm sure you know I represent Emily Henderson."

She took a long sip of her drink and nodded.

"What was your relationship with Philip Barnes?"

Taylor smiled. "You get right to the point. I like that. Philip and I were 'very good friends'."

"I understand he was moving from the house he shared with Nancy Osborne. Was he moving in with you?"

She almost choked on her drink. "You've got to be kidding."

Coulter raised an eyebrow. "You mean he wasn't?"

Taylor leaned back on her barstool. She finished her drink and poured another. She motioned to his glass. He shook his head.

"Coulter, I am forty-nine years old with very few illusions. I have a great deal of money, which I intend to keep. I met Philip a couple of months ago when he delivered a chair which Nancy Osborne had repaired for me. I liked what I saw."

Coulter nodded.

"I had him checked out. He was single, had been a police officer for ten years, and as they say, clean. Our relationship was strictly physical. I don't intend to become emotionally involved with anyone. I prefer a casual relationship with no strings and no ties."

"When I interviewed Nancy Osborne, she told me that she had asked Philip to move out," Coulter said.

Taylor shook her head. "Nancy's a drug addict and was crazy about Philip. He mentioned she threatened to kill him if he left. Of course, he may have been exaggerating."

"I've had the questionable pleasure of meeting her. I'd bet Philip was telling the truth," Coulter replied.

Taylor laughed. "It sounds like she came on to you. Nancy isn't too subtle. With her looks, she can't afford to be."

"Tell me, Taylor, do you know of anyone with a motive for killing Philip?"

"Cops always make enemies. Nancy might have killed him, though I doubt it. The day before Philip was killed, he laughed and told me he had received two death threats. He thought it was funny."

"Did Philip ever mention his work?"

"No." She smiled. "We didn't talk a lot."

"I am sure you are glad to be out of the relationship. I believe someone hired him and his partner to kill Emily Henderson, and we now know they murdered Clarice Weitzel's daughter, Laurie."

"Clarice is an old friend. For a while, I didn't think she would get through it. She turned her life around by starting the Center."

Taylor seemed lost in thought for several minutes before turning back to Coulter.

"Do you think the attempt to kill Emily could have anything to do with the sale of one section of her mineral rights to our company?"

Coulter was stunned. "Excuse me? What are you talking about?"

"With the oil crisis, we have been buying up West Texas land which is rich in natural gas. Emily Henderson owns the mineral rights to a great deal of land adjacent to a recent strike.

"While I was out of the country, one of my executives contacted her husband regarding the purchase of some of those mineral rights."

"All of this is news to me, as I am sure it is to Emily." Coulter said. "How much money are we talking about?"

"More than half a million dollars, probably closer to six-hundred-thousand dollars."

"Your company has been negotiating with Mr. Henderson?"

"Not me, personally. I would know better, with your client's divorce pending. One of the reasons I came to town was to contact you, since you are her attorney. Supposedly, her husband has power of attorney, which I'm sure you and I will be checking out immediately. Looks like he figured he would grab her money before she found out about the sale. He sounds like a real sweet guy."

Coulter nodded. "You can say that again. Emily has no idea about any pending sale, and to my knowledge, Dan has no power of attorney."

"I'm so glad we've talked. I'm anxious to conclude the matter. I hope you will tell Emily that I play fair, and to please feel free to have me checked out."

Coulter nodded. "You have a reputation for being fair but tough. I'll talk with her this evening and get back to you in the next day or two. You have given me a possible motive for the attempt on Emily's life, and the two murders. It has been a very enlightening conversation, to say the least."

"I have already talked to my executive." Taylor smiled. "If he wasn't my son, I'd have fired him. There will be no further negotiations between Taylor Oil and Gas and Dan Henderson."

"One more thing, Taylor. I don't want Dan to know we're on to him. If he tries to contact your company again, could everyone be unavailable for a few days?"

"You can count on it."

Coulter set his still-full glass on the bar and got up to go. "It has been a real pleasure meeting you, Taylor, and I mean that sincerely."

"Thank you. I wish you good luck. For what it's worth, I think she's innocent, too."

33

Coulter drove directly to Parkland. He'd called ahead, and Emily was waiting for him when he arrived. He took her hands in his. "You know the saying 'I have some good news and some bad news'?"

Emily laughed. "I can tell the good news is something you're bursting to tell me. Before you do, I have some good news of my own. I've started dreaming about the night before the murders. I know I'm getting close to remembering everything. Now tell me your news."

"Why don't we sit down?"

"Hmm. Sounds ominous."

"The mineral rights your grandfather left you. I believe you said it was in a trust. How is it set up?"

"Oh, it's not really a trust. The deeds to the mineral rights are in a safe deposit box at First Bank in Abilene. My grandfather's lawyer, Mr. Jeffers, contacts me when someone wants to purchase any of the rights. Both Mr. Jeffers and I have to sign in to access the safe deposit box. If I agree to sell, Mr. Jeffers prepares the necessary documents after I give him the original deed. I deposit the money I receive in my separate account at First Bank."

"Does Dan have your power of attorney?" Coulter asked.

"No. Why? What's the matter?"

"I've just come from an interview with Taylor Niedringhaus. She owns Taylor Oil and Gas. Some of the mineral rights you inherited from your grandfather are adjacent to one of their gas strikes in West Texas. If you decide to sell, the amount is over a half-million dollars."

Emily laughed. "What do you mean—_if_ I decide to sell!"

"While Taylor was out of the Country, her company executive was negotiating with Dan. He represented himself as having your power of attorney, probably forged your signature. Taylor put a stop to it as soon as she returned.

"The bad news is we may have the reason for your attempted murder. I believe Dan and Wanda wanted you dead so Dan would inherit all of your money."

Emily stared at him and held up her hand for him to stop. "Wait a minute. You are telling me the good news is I am rich, and the bad news is my husband tried to have me killed?"

"I guess I shouldn't have blurted it out as I did."

"No, you shouldn't have." She sighed. "I guess you had to tell me sometime."

"I know it is a lot to take in. I need to prepare papers for Mrs. Niedringhaus's company, if you decide to sell. She would like to wrap up the transaction as soon as possible. I'll have Johnny check to make certain Taylor's offer is in line."

Emily tried to smile. "Are you kidding! You bet I'll sell. After all, I have a lawyer to pay for saving my life."

Coulter shook his head. "The important thing is to nail Dan and Wanda. I haven't had time to figure out how to prove they are guilty, but I promise I will."

"Now we know why Dan didn't want a divorce. If we were divorced, he would only receive half the money."

"If that's what he thought, he'd be wrong. The property you inherited before you were married is not community property. He would receive nothing. It may explain why the cops were killed. You were set up to take the fall and receive the death penalty. Unless you changed your will, Dan would inherit."

Emily shook her head. "I know Dan was cold and uncaring after the assault. It's hard for me to believe he would have me killed. I guess it shows what a good judge of character I am."

"Sometimes money does crazy things to someone who is otherwise a decent person. I'll prepare the papers tonight so I can concentrate on Dan and Wanda. I suggest we set up the documents to require both our signatures to prevent any more forgeries." He glanced down at her as he stood up to go. She looked so sad. Before he realized what he was doing, he kissed her forehead. "Will you be okay, or would you like Mary to come by?"

"Thanks. I'd rather be alone."

After Coulter had gone and Emily was back in her room, she replayed her conversation with Coulter. Dan had been her whole life. How could she deal with this kind of betrayal? She practiced deep breathing and tried to think what Mary's advice would be.

Emily decided Mary would say to allow herself to feel sad, then accept it and move on. Dwelling on it was pointless and damaging. Emily relaxed and fell into a deep sleep.

• • • • • •

When Coulter turned into his driveway, his headlights lit up the lawn leading down to the lake. He saw Mary stretched out on a blanket, enjoying the cool Fall air. He walked over and dropped down beside her.

"I am glad you are home," she said. "This has been a very eventful day for you, hasn't it?"

He didn't bother to ask how she knew.

"Yeah." He filled her in on the details.

"Lowell stopped by earlier. He gave me a message for you. 'Tell Coulter it's time to either fish or cut bait'."

"We go to trial in six days. Lowell deserves an answer tomorrow. I have no idea how to prove Dan and Wanda are responsible for Emily's attempted murder and the murder of the cops. I've run out of time. Any ideas?"

Mary touched his cheek. "No one can help you. We have talked before about a person's time of testing. This is also a time of testing for you. During my meditation, I was told to give you this information. Dan Henderson had nothing to do with the attempt on Emily's life, nor does he have any idea who is responsible. He also knows nothing about the murders of the two policemen."

Coulter could only stare at her. Dan Henderson was innocent? He didn't doubt Mary's information for a minute. But what the hell was he going to do now? He'd hurt Emily by telling her of his theory regarding Dan. He held her life in his hands and he felt it slipping through his fingers.

34

The phone rang as Coulter walked into his office the next morning.

"Morning, McBride, it's Lowell. Glad I caught you."

Coulter laughed. "Mary gave me your message. There have been several developments. I plan to give you Mrs. Henderson's answer tomorrow."

"Actually, I'm calling about something else. It might make your client's decision a little easier."

"Like what?"

"I'm getting ready to interview a witness. Ordinarily, I would just give you her name on my witness list. I thought you would like to hear what she has to say first-hand."

"When and where?" Coulter asked.

"I thought we would meet at your office. Mine has a lot of eyes and ears. This afternoon all right with you?"

"Sure."

"The lady's name is Alice Bartlett. See you around two o'clock." Lowell hung up.

Coulter knew Emily was in serious trouble. Lowell's witness must know something so incriminating that Lowell figured it would force them to take his deal.

. . . . .

Coulter watched Lowell pull into the driveway and help a pleasant-looking woman out of the car. She looked to be around sixty years old, and she moved like someone who spent a lot of time on her feet.

They crossed the patio and Coulter went out to meet them. "Hello, Lowell," Coulter said.

"Mrs. Bartlett, this is Coulter McBride," Lowell introduced them. Coulter shook her hand. "Nice to meet you, Mrs. Bartlett. Please come on in."

As they went inside, Mrs. Bartlett looked around. "My, what a pretty room. I feel like I'm still outside."

"Thank you. Please have a seat. This chair has a nice view of the lake." He motioned Lowell to sit behind his desk.

Coulter walked to a table with cups and glasses he had set out earlier and took some bottles of water from the refrigerator. "Would you like anything to drink?"

"Water would be nice," Mrs. Bartlett replied.

Lowell nodded and Coulter poured three bottles of water into glasses. He settled in a chair across from Mrs. Bartlett.

Lowell took charge of the meeting. "Mrs. Bartlett called me regarding some information she has about your client's case. This is just an informal discussion. I will ask her a few questions, and if you think of anything more, Coulter, just let me know. We'll take a formal statement later if needed."

"Mrs. Bartlett, where are you employed?" Lowell began.

Mrs. Bartlett brushed back a strand of gray hair with a large, work-worn hand.

"Jay's Coffee Shop."

"You work the night shift. Is that correct?"

She nodded. "Eleven p.m. to seven a.m. for the past twenty years."

"What is the address of Jay's Coffee Shop?"

"It's on the corner of Marsh Lane and Forest, 2001 Forest Lane."

"How far would you say Jay's Coffee Shop is from Harry Hines and Royal Lane?"

"Let me see. You would go west on Forest to Harry Hines, that's about twelve blocks, turn left and go about three or four blocks to where Royal Lane crosses. It's about five minutes away."

Lowell glanced at Coulter. "Mrs. Bartlett, have you ever seen Mrs. Henderson before you saw this picture of her in the paper?"

Mrs. Bartlett looked at the picture, then returned her gaze to Lowell. "Yes, sir."

"And when was that, please?"

Coulter's face flushed. He could guess what was coming.

"It was a little before two o'clock the morning of September 5th."

"Was she alone?"

Mrs. Bartlett nodded. "Oh, yes. The poor little thing. I remember she was shivering, and I brought her two pots of tea. Her face looked like she had been in an accident. I asked if she was okay, and she just smiled and nodded. She stayed about half an hour. I remember she left me a nice tip."

"She left Jay's Coffee Shop around two-thirty in the morning?" Lowell asked.

"Yes, sir, and I never saw her again until her picture."

"Thank you, Mrs. Bartlett. I don't have any more questions right now. I explained you may have to appear at the trial."

"Yes, sir, I understand."

Lowell turned to Coulter. "Do you have any questions for Mrs. Bartlett?"

"None I can think of. If Mrs. Bartlett has no objection, I would like to have a picture of her for my file. Maybe outside on the patio."

Lowell turned to Mrs. Bartlett, who smiled and nodded.

"Fine," Lowell said. "You can make a copy for me as well."

Coulter took his Polaroid from a desk drawer and walked with them outside to the patio. Mrs. Bartlett smiled, and he quickly took two shots.

Lowell nodded to Coulter. "Talk to you this afternoon."

Coulter watched them leave. How could he have been so stupid? He had bought Emily's story. He wanted a drink. Instead, he got into his car and headed for Parkland.

35

Emily looked up as Coulter entered the Parkland visitors' room. "I didn't know who was coming when the matron brought me down. I wasn't expecting to see you again so soon, but I'm happy you're here. You must have those papers for me to sign." Then she saw the expression on his face. "What's wrong? Don't tell me it's more bad news."

Coulter was so angry he had to force himself not to yell. "You might say it is good news and bad news again." He threw the pictures of Mrs. Bartlett across the table and sat down.

"Ever see her before?"

Emily picked up the pictures and stared at them for several minutes. She caught her breath as a series of images flashed across her mind. She closed her eyes, trying to sort them out.

"I'm waiting. Have you ever seen her before?" Coulter demanded.

She cringed before his anger. "Yes."

"Where?"

"At a restaurant the morning of the murders."

"What in the hell were you doing there?" he shouted.

Emily looked him in the eye. "I didn't remember I was there. Little things started coming back to me. I mentioned it to you yesterday when you told me that Dan tried to have me killed. There were only bits and pieces before. Just now when I studied the woman's picture, I remembered her and it all fell into place."

"Don't give me that crap!" he snapped.

Emily gave him a hurt look before she continued. "I was half out of my mind that morning. I woke up at the lake house and got this crazy idea to follow Hunter and Barnes to make sure they didn't hurt anyone else. I remember calling to see if they were on duty." Her eyes were pleading.

He ignored her. "You gave me your promise. Remember? No matter how bad it was, no lies!"

Emily's voice was calm. "I did not lie before, and I am not lying now."

"God, Emily, we promised to tell each other the truth, no matter what. I feel so betrayed."

Her eyes flashed as she leaned across the table. "Well, how do you like it, mister? It doesn't feel real good, does it? Whether you believe me or not, I did not betray you."

Coulter ran a hand through his hair. "I'm sorry. It was the last thing I was thinking about when Lowell let me have it with both barrels."

His voice when he spoke again was normal. "Did you witness the murders?" Coulter could not believe it until he heard his own words. He had asked her if she had witnessed the murders, not if she'd killed them.

"Coulter! Of course not."

"Why couldn't you trust me enough to tell me you were there?" he asked again.

Emily looked at him as she reached for his hand. "I will say it one more time. I did not remember until just now. Let me ask you a question about trust. Would you have thought it possible I was there and didn't kill them?"

"I don't—yes, I would," he replied at last.

"Coulter, you believed in me. The miracle is, I know you still do."

"How long did you follow them?" His voice was gentle now as he kept her hand.

Her eyes widened. "I didn't. The fog was too thick. I went directly from the diner to the Center. I slept in the car and drove to my house the next morning, where they arrested me."

"I almost forgot about the good news," Coulter said.

"I didn't kill them. It has to be the best news I will ever receive in my life."

Coulter sighed. "Mary was home when I arrived last night. She said in her meditation she was instructed to tell me that Dan was not involved in the attempt to kill you or to kill the cops. I was wrong. He is innocent of everything except trying to steal your money."

Emily dropped her head. "I'm sorry about your theory, but I can't help being glad Dan didn't try to have me killed."

He put his hand gently under her chin and raised her head until she was looking at him. "I'm glad, too." Coulter put his arm around her and she relaxed into the strength of him.

"I know it looks bad," Emily said. "Tell Lowell we can't accept his offer. If something goes wrong and I'm convicted, I would rather be dead than spend the rest of my life in prison. There are worse things than dying. Believe me, I know."

Coulter nodded. "I'm not sure how I am going to prepare for trial. The papers are ready for your signature so you can get on with the deal with Taylor's company." He searched his pockets and laughed. "I'll have to call the matron for a pen." He laughed. "I don't have a pen. No lawyer is ever without a pen!"

"That's one battle we've won," Emily said, smiling. "Dan is really going to be surprised. I would love to see the look on his face. Now we're ready for the next one."

"I'm so close to proving who is behind everything. I just can't figure a way."

Emily grinned. "To borrow a favorite phrase of someone very dear to me, 'Don't worry. It ain't over with yet'."

36

Coulter picked up the phone and dialed. "Marshall Lowell," came the voice on the other end of the line.

"How's it going?" Coulter asked.

"I've been waiting for your call. What did Mrs. Henderson decide?"

"She is not taking your deal. We'll see you in court. Emily Henderson's not guilty, Lowell, so unless I can give you the guilty party or parties, we'll be rolling the dice."

There was a long pause on the other end of the line. "She really is crazy. There is no way you can possibly win. You know it, Coulter. I gave you a break by sharing Mrs. Bartlett's information with you, hoping you would take the deal."

"I know, and I do appreciate it. I told you the other night I believe Emily's innocent. I still do. I didn't try to change her mind because I believe she is doing the right thing."

Coulter sighed. "I'm pretty sure who is behind this whole mess. I just have to figure a way to prove it. Maybe I'll be able to tie it up in a red ribbon for you before trial starts."

"This isn't what a prosecutor usually says, but good luck. And I really mean it."

• • • • •

It was dusk when Coulter arrived home. He went directly to his office without bothering to turn on any lights. Soc seemed to realize something was wrong and lay down at Coulter's feet, instead of jumping onto his lap as he usually did.

Coulter took the half-gallon bottle of Wellers from the bar and set it on the desk in front of him. Chin in hand, he stared at the bottle for a long time. He slowly removed the cap and picked up a glass. He held the glass in his hand, then set it back down.

He leaned back in his chair, unable to stop the kaleidoscope of his investigation from flashing through his mind. What was he missing? There had to be a way. He again picked up the bottle of whiskey. Suddenly, his jaw clenched, and he hurried to the sink. He made himself a drink and poured the rest down the drain.

He propped his feet on the desk and stared through the glass ceiling at the stars popping out in the clear night. An idea came to him so preposterous he laughed out loud. It was so absurd it just might work. He grabbed a yellow pad and started mapping out his strategy.

37

Emily watched the sun come up through her barred window. Unable to sleep, she had practiced her yoga and breathing exercises. She had spent the rest of the night in meditation. Monday her trial would begin. Monday was also her twenty-first birthday—the beginning of a new year and maybe the beginning of a new life.

· · · · ·

Emily could hardly wait for Mary's arrival at Parkland. She looked up as Mary came into the visitors' room.

Mary hugged her, then held her back to look at her. "I see you have some good news to tell me."

"Oh, Mary, I've remembered everything. I didn't kill them. I finally know I am innocent. It is the best news I could ever have."

Mary nodded. "Yes, you are radiating different energy. Now you are ready to face anything." She sat down across from Emily and, as usual, slid off her moccasins.

"Coulter asked me to bring you some clothes to wear in case you go to trial. I told Coulter there will not be a trial. At least not the kind they have in courts. You are in the middle of your fight to regain your personal power, which is your real trial."

Emily sighed. "I'm relieved my old life is almost over—win or lose. Somehow, I know we will win, though I have no idea how." She fingered her orange outfit. "It will be wonderful to get out of these." She reached for Mary's hand. "It is vitally important for Coulter to win my case, isn't it? Not only for me, but for him."

"Yes."

"Mary, please tell me about Coulter."

"What would you like to know?"

"Anything. Everything. You raised him and know him better than anyone."

"Coulter is a good man, and very sensitive. There is the Irish melancholy. They say no one can suffer like the Irish." Mary grinned. "The Cherokee half forces him to suffer in silence."

"Something terrible happened, and it almost destroyed him?"

Mary's black eyes stared through her, then she nodded. "I think it is time you knew."

Emily took Mary's hand. "I can't hide anything from you. You obviously know how I feel about him."

Mary was silent for several minutes. Finally, she started her story. "A young man robbed a convenience store, killed the store clerk and two customers. The Court appointed Coulter to defend him. This young man was without conscience and bragged to him about the murders. The jury would have found him guilty. Coulter discovered something about the search and seizure, which was illegal. If he told District Attorney Lowell, the Court would have no choice. The man would go free."

"What a terrible position to be in."

"Yes. He agonized over his decision. He discussed the matter with his father, who said 'the law is the law. You know what you must do'."

"His father persuaded him to reveal the technicality?"

"Emily, sometimes we are given awareness of what fate has in store when we are given an important choice to make. I believe Coulter's father had this awareness. He made the choice for Coulter, knowing what the cost would be to them both."

"I don't understand."

Mary touched her finger to Emily's lips. "Coulter carried a lot of guilt because of his decision. He felt responsible for letting a murderer go free. He knew people killed for many reasons, but believed circumstances provoked most people and killed only once in their life. But he knew this man would kill again.

"About three months later," Mary continued, "Coulter's father was driving back from Fort Worth. It was around midnight. He stopped at a convenience store because Coulter had asked if he would mind picking up a pack of cigarettes for him on his way home. A young man entered the store, pulled a gun, and demanded money.

"The clerk gave him all the money in the drawer. Coulter's father gave up his wallet. It made no difference. The young man shot them both. The clerk lived. Coulter's father did not."

"Oh, no!"

"The man who murdered his father was the same man who Coulter had set free. He blamed himself, of course. It changed him as nothing else in the world could have."

"How could he bear it?" Emily cried.

"Alcohol was his crutch the first year. He never left his house until the second. Slowly, he began his way back."

"It explains so much."

"There are those who would call it an impossible coincidence, except there is no such thing as coincidence. It was already written, just as your trial-by-fire was already written, as is your fate. I believe Coulter has come to understand this—at least the Indian part of him has. I am not so sure about the Irish."

"I have one question."

Mary waited, already knowing what she would be asked.

"Why were you not able to help him?"

"At the beginning, he would talk to no one. I had to wait until he was ready. He and I talked for many hours. He had to work through his pain and grief to the bottom of his soul in his own way. Your way was different.

"There is a universal rule, Emily. *You can never be responsible for another human being. We are not allowed to interfere with another's path.* It is very painful to watch a loved one stumble and fall. You can only be there for them and give your love and support. The rest is up to them."

"So everyone walks their path alone."

Mary shook her head. "No, Emily. No one is ever alone."

38

Coulter listened to the rain blowing hard against the glass roof and windows. The cigarette in his hand burned down, unnoticed, until he became aware of the heat and dropped it into an ashtray. His slacks and rumpled shirt looked as if he had slept in them, which he had.

Scribbled notes, papers, and books were spread over the room. The cold tile floor felt good against his bare feet as he went to the refrigerator to retrieve a carton of milk. He poured a glass for himself and a saucer for Soc, who had nipped at Coulter's ankle and mewed for his share.

He switched off the lamp and sat in the darkness, lit another cigarette, and watched the lightning illuminate the sky. Soc padded noiselessly across the floor and jumped onto his lap. He absentmindedly stroked the cat's head.

Monday the battle would begin. In the old days, he would have loved a trial like this one. Not anymore. He had prepared the papers needed for his plan to trap the killer and prove Emily's innocence, but what if it didn't work? He shook his head to dispel the thought and headed for the shower.

39

Mary Setting Sun was in deep meditation. Suddenly her eyes opened wide. She cleaned her hands and face with cedar smoke coming from the fireplace, found her moccasins, and headed for Parkland.

Emily walked slowly into Parkland's visitors' room, where she had spent so much time. Her eyes were clear and her manner composed. She was surprised to see Mary was waiting for her.

"I told you at the beginning you were being tested," Mary said. "You have succeeded in cleansing your mind. The most crucial test is immediately before you. The choice you make will decide your future and Coulter's, though he believes it is he who holds your future in his hands.

"You will be required to make a leap of faith, trust without question, put your ego aside, forgive, and be willing to give up everything. I do not know what the test will be, except the outcome is of vital importance."

"Give up everything?" Emily smiled. "The only thing I have to give up is money, and it's of no importance."

"That is all the news I have for you today." Mary hugged her and left.

When Emily rang for the matron, she was advised another visitor had arrived. So this would be their trial-by-fire.

She knew it would be Coulter. She looked up as he entered the room. She saw how his eyes sparkled and she felt a surge of hope. Coulter went over his conversations with Tiffany and Taylor again.

"What does it all mean, and how does it affect anything?" Emily asked. "We don't have any kind of proof of who the murderer is."

"Well, we know who it's not. I have a plan. It is a long shot and everything depends upon you."

Emily nodded. "Mary was just here to tell me that she saw this happening. What do you want me to do?"

Coulter explained his plan. When he finished he waited, suddenly afraid she would refuse. "I know I'm asking a lot of you. It's your decision, Emily."

"I agree with you. It is my only chance."

"You are sure you want to go for it?"

"Absolutely!"

Coulter took some papers from his briefcase and handed them to her.

"You will need to sign these. This one gives me your power of attorney. This is to advise Mr. Jeffers to fax the documents which Mrs. Niedringhaus will need."

Emily signed the papers as he handed them to her without reading them. After she finished, she leaned back in her chair. "Know the first thing I want to do when I'm free?"

Coulter noticed she didn't say "if". "Just name it."

Emily giggled. "I want to go on a picnic."

"I know just the place. My house faces White Rock Lake. I'll get some outrageously expensive snacks from Marty's and some of their best wine."

"We'll sit in the sun and listen to the water. I assume you have ducks on your lake?"

Coulter nodded. "There is a ritual my father started years ago. Every morning we used to spread food on our lake side for the birds and ducks, and any other animals who happened by."

"With the meditations Mary taught me, I've learned to visualize the aroma of honeysuckle, the way cut grass smells, and how gravel feels under my bare feet. I can taste ice-cold beer trickling down my throat as I bite into a hot dog and feel the sun on my face. Soon I will experience all those things again."

He shook off the fear of his plan failing. It would be a desperate gamble. It was their only hope.

Coulter kissed her cheek. "Wish me luck."

40

Coulter headed for Taylor's office at Elm and Griffin. He disliked driving downtown through the upper portion of the "corridor" as Elm, Main, and Commerce Streets were known. The upper corridor, once the action center of downtown, was now pretty much abandoned, with empty buildings that once housed busy offices with workers and shoppers scurrying around. Of the department stores, only the original Neiman Marcus remained at Main and Ervay Streets.

Once he hit Griffin Street, the area came alive. The federal and state courthouses were busy, as always.

Taylor's office was in the "green building" at Elm and Griffin, filled mostly with large prestigious law firms doing business in the courthouses. The name had changed over the years, according to the bank that owned it. It didn't matter. Everyone referred to it as the green building because bright green lights surrounded the entire seventy stories.

It was a landmark, taking the place of the flying red horse. It stood out in the night sky and was always pictured on TV shots of downtown.

Unfortunately, it only offered public parking. Coulter reluctantly parked the Caddy in an open lot across the street where the attendant was stacking the cars four and five deep. He handed the attendant an extra twenty dollars to let him park the car himself at a spot reserved for a fast getaway.

He took the elevator to the 60th floor and stepped out into a plush reception area with oak inlaid floors peeking out from expensive Persian carpets.

He returned the smile of the blond at the reception desk.

"I'm Coulter McBride. I believe Mrs. Niedringhaus is expecting me."

She whispered into the phone as if it was a secret and turned back to Coulter. "Please have a seat. Mrs. Niedringhaus will be with you shortly."

Taylor strode into the reception area a few minutes later. She wore all black—figure-hugging jeans and a gorgeous suede top which accentuated her black and silver hair. Her snakeskin boots completed the outfit. Not exactly business attire, but if you were Taylor Niedringhaus, you didn't have to give a damn. Besides, she looked great.

Her smile was wide, and her eyes twinkled. "Hi."

"Hi, yourself," Coulter replied.

"Looks like you're ready to rumble."

He followed her into an office that had Taylor's stamp all over it. An Indian blanket was draped over a well-worn black leather couch across from matching leather chairs, with a working-size table in between.

Remington's *End of the Trail* graced the credenza behind an oak desk, which Coulter guessed was her father's, and was now Taylor's. A grainy black-and-white picture of an older man and young girl standing in front of a spewing oil well hung behind the couch. Taylor followed Coulter's glance.

"I like to remember where it all began," she said.

A storm was rolling in. Glancing out one of the floor-to-ceiling windows, Coulter could look down at the fast-moving dark clouds. "Being in the middle of the clouds is a spooky feeling," he said. "I wouldn't want to hang around here if tornado warnings were out."

"I've only had to walk down sixty flights of stairs once. What gets to me is hearing the columns, or whatever they are, creaking. You can actually feel the building move. I prefer both feet on the ground." She motioned him to a chair and took the other one.

Some documents lay on the table. "Emily's mineral releases were delivered this morning," Taylor said. "This is the one I'm currently interested in, though in looking them over, I may be negotiating for more. I'll keep them all in the safe if it's okay with you?"

"Fine." Coulter opened his briefcase and handed her the power of attorney and the signed bill of sale he and Emily had executed.

Taylor looked them over and smiled. "Great. I'll have copies of everything made for you." She stood. "Shall we head upstairs to Executive Banking? The money should be ready for you. Do you mind if I ask what you have planned?"

"We're going to give it away, or at least part of it."

"You have the same look my dad used to get when a gusher was about to come in."

"Pretty good analogy," Coulter replied.

They took the elevator to the 65th floor. The reception area was hushed, as if only the biggest transactions took place here.

Taylor walked past the receptionist and headed for an office large enough to get lost in. She tapped on the open door and a portly man in a navy suit, white banker's shirt and subdued tie rose to meet them. His manner was deferential as he smiled at her.

Coulter suspected a lot of bankers treated her this way. It was completely lost on Taylor.

"Hello, Bernard," she said. "Coulter, this is Bernard Marston."

Coulter nodded, and they shook hands.

"Is everything ready?" Taylor asked.

"Of course," Marston replied. He opened a black suitcase and handed it to Coulter, along with a document to review and sign.

The case contained six-hundred-thousand dollars in stacks of banded bills. Coulter didn't insult Marston by counting the money.

Marston smiled. "The suitcase is on the house."

Coulter guessed for six-hundred-thousand dollars he could afford it.

"Thanks, Bernard," Taylor said. "We have to get going." She started out of the room.

Coulter smiled at Bernard and followed Taylor into the elevator. She punched her floor and the ground floor for him.

"Would you do me a favor?" she asked.

"Name it."

"When it's over, will you tell me the whole story?"

"You've got it, and thanks for everything, Taylor."

"No reason to thank me. It's a win-win situation."

41

The Caddy was just as he had left it. Coulter was running on adrenaline when he arrived at Dan Henderson's home. The Honda was parked in the driveway.

Dan was dressed in a suit and tie, his blond hair perfectly coiffed. His eyes narrowed when he recognized his caller.

"Hello, Dan, mind if I come in?"

Dan was at a loss for words, though he recovered quickly. "What the hell are you doing here?"

"I have a deal for you," Coulter replied.

"Yeah? What kind of deal would you be making with me?"

"Why don't you invite me in and find out?"

Dan shrugged and held open the door. Coulter followed him into the den, set the black suitcase on the coffee table, and sat down on the couch.

"Okay," Dan snapped, "let's have it."

Coulter flipped the locks on the case. "Ever see six-hundred-thousand dollars at one time?"

Dan eyed him suspiciously as he shook his head.

Coulter opened the case and turned it around.

Dan's eyes were slits. "You have my money from the mineral rights."

"Correction. I have Emily's money from the mineral rights. We are aware you tried to steal it. Good news, Dan. There is a way you can get back some or all of it."

"Don't mess with me, shyster. You hate my guts. Why would you be giving me a red dime?"

"Easy. You're gonna catch a murderer for me and you'll be well paid for it."

"Okay, wise guy, what's your story? It had better be good."

"I don't believe you were involved in the plan to kill Emily."

"Of course not," Dan sputtered. "Surely you can't believe I was?"

"You said the story had better be good. Well it is, my friend. You probably bragged to Wanda about the mineral rights. Your sweet little Wanda hired Hunter and Barnes to kill Emily to get her hands on the money. When her little scheme didn't work, she murdered them to keep them quiet, but primarily to put the blame on Emily—so she would get the death penalty and you would get it all."

"You're crazy as hell, shyster. Why would Wanda do anything like that? Half the money would be mine from the divorce. You know, community property."

Coulter smiled. "Wanda said she liked men who were not too smart. The trust was set up long before you and Emily were married. Wanda was well aware that it wasn't community property. The only way she, through you, could get her hands on the money was to kill Emily."

"Wanda could never do anything like that. You're crazy!"

"Am I?" Coulter leaned back on the couch. "Okay, here's the deal. Either way it goes, it's a sweet deal for you."

Dan pursed his lips. "What do I have to do?"

"I want you to call Wanda. Tell her you got your hands on the money before Emily found out about it. Make sure she knows it is six-hundred-thousand dollars. You might want to brag about how you outsmarted the bank because you had a power of attorney.

"Wanda may be a little suspicious. I figure after killing two people to get her hands on the money, she won't be able to resist."

"Resist what? This is some kind of trick. You can't make me believe you are going to give me six-hundred-thousand dollars. You're dangling it like a carrot, then you'll pull it away."

Coulter sighed. "Emily has agreed to the plan. It's her money, of course. I'll lay it out for you, and it ain't pretty. If Wanda had nothing to do with the attempt to kill Emily or the cop murders, you and Wanda get the six-hundred-thousand dollars.

"If you help us prove Wanda's guilty, half of the six-hundred-thousand is yours. Personally, I think Wanda will try to kill you to get her hands on all the money. She has no intention of splitting it with you."

Dan laughed. "You really are crazy. Wanda loves me."

"Then prove it, stud. Call Wanda and have her come to your house after the bar closes. Tell her the two of you must disappear tomorrow. Make sure she knows the money is in cash.

"Tell her now that you have the money, all you want is her. She'll believe it. Wanda thinks she is irresistible. I am confident you will be convincing. Make sure you insist the two of you have to leave tomorrow before Emily or I find out about the money."

Dan reached across the coffee table, pulled the suitcase onto his lap, and leafed through the money. He smiled. "What happens if Wanda's innocent?"

"Then you get the bundle."

"What if Wanda wants the money but not me?"

Coulter arched an eyebrow. "I thought you said she loved you."

"She does."

"This is the beauty of your deal," Coulter said as he took a sheet of paper from an envelope and handed it to Dan.

"It's an agreement signed by Emily. It spells out what I just explained. If Wanda's guilty—whether or not she tries to kill you—half the money still belongs to you. Like it says on the notarized paper, for services rendered, three-hundred-thousand dollars."

"How do I know this isn't a trick?"

The hint of a smile played on Coulter's lips. He had him. "Easy. Take the money and the signed agreement with you. Only I wouldn't let Wanda see the document if I were you."

Dan began to pace the room. "I know you're wrong about Wanda. If you're not, will I be protected?"

"Damned right. Johnny's licensed to carry a gun. You don't think I would trust you not to take off with the whole six-hundred-thousand, do you? Anyway, you are our only chance of saving Emily and somewhere deep down, I think you still have a little decency left."

"Okay. I'm in," Dan said at last.

"You have to agree to the house being wired. We are doing this by the book. Try to stay in the den. Johnny will have a few extra gadgets around besides the wiring. Does Wanda ever park in your garage?"

Dan shook his head. "There's no room."

"Okay. Johnny and I will set up there."

Dan picked up the suitcase again and stared at the money. "You're on, and you're gonna look real stupid when Wanda and me are on our way with six-hundred grand." He frowned, then turned back to Coulter. "What makes you think I won't tell Wanda about the deal?"

Coulter laughed. "Easy, again. Johnny will be right with you until Wanda arrives. He will make sure you don't try any secret phone calls. If you try to signal her after she arrives? With a great deal of pleasure, I'll convince Wanda you set her up, and that, my friend, I believe will cause you to end up very, very dead."

42

Coulter pulled into the parking lot of Spring Creek Barbeque. A breeze carried the wonderful aroma to him as soon as he stepped out of the car. He went through the cafeteria-style serving line for ribs, baked beans, and coleslaw.

He spotted Bannister devouring ribs with sauce-covered fingers. Coulter set his tray down across the table. "Hey, Lou."

"Oh, Oh. You didn't call me flatfoot. You must need a really big favor to be tracking me down."

"You couldn't be more wrong. I have a gift for you."

Bannister smiled at the young lady passing out hot yeast rolls from a napkin-covered basket. She handed each of them two.

"Oh, how I love these," Bannister said around a mouthful of buttered roll. "Okay, what's the gift?"

"You're going to get credit for catching Hunter's and Barnes' killer."

"If memory serves, she is currently residing at Parkland, unless she's escaped."

"Come on, you and I both know Emily didn't kill anyone. We are going to prove it, with help from Johnny Tompkins and Dan Henderson."

"Good grief. That poor excuse for a man?"

"Yeah, I know. It's going down tonight. Johnny's babysitting Henderson as we speak."

Bannister downed his second roll. "Okay. Let's have it."

He listened without interrupting as Coulter outlined his plan. When Coulter finished, Bannister smiled. "I always thought Emily had a lot of class—and guts. She also has to have a lot of faith in her lawyer."

"So, what do you think?"

Bannister caught the girl's eye and signaled for another roll. "I think we should do a little more planning."

43

Sweat ran down Dan Henderson's face as he watched Johnny wire every room and add video equipment in the den. Wanda had agreed to come by when the bar closed. Coulter and Johnny set up headquarters in the garage.

Dan was afraid Wanda would somehow see the wires. After searching, even he couldn't spot them. He spent the night pacing and looking at his watch and driving Coulter crazy. At midnight, Johnny took over and Coulter gratefully took a nap.

At four o'clock, Dan went out to the garage. "McBride, something's wrong. She should have been here by now."

"Relax. She'll be here."

"What if she doesn't come?" Dan whined.

"If you don't get back in the house, I am going to punch you out and we will drag you to the couch."

"I'm going. I'm going." Dan closed the garage door and returned to the den after pouring himself another bourbon.

Wanda's car pulled into the driveway at dawn. Johnny joined Coulter in the garage.

"I was beginning to think you weren't coming," Dan said as he tried to kiss her.

"I got held up." She stepped away from him. "What's the matter with you? You're sweating like a pig."

"I'm afraid of getting caught with the money, and I've been waiting up all night for you."

"Uh, uh. I can read you like a damned book. Come on, tell mama all about it." Her eyes narrowed. "You've got the money, haven't you?"

Dan forced a smile. "Yeah. Listen, we gotta get out of town. The banker seemed suspicious. I'm afraid he checked with McBride."

"Relax. You're being paranoid. We've got all the time in the world." She pressed her body against his. "What you need is a little lovin'." She pulled him down onto the couch. "Yeah, mama knows exactly what you need."

"Not now, sweetheart. I'm telling you we gotta leave."

Wanda made a face. "Stop your damned whining, you little coward." She got up and smoothed her clothes. "Come on, show me the money."

Dan took the suitcase from the closet. Wanda grabbed it out of his hands and opened it, oblivious to everything else. She ran her hands through the bills. "It is finally mine."

"You mean ours," Dan replied. "We've got to disappear today."

Wanda's disgust showed on her face. "I never realized you were so gutless. I'm not running from anybody."

"I thought we would head for San Francisco," Dan went on as if he hadn't heard her. "You've always talked about going there."

Wanda's eyes gleamed as she fondled the money. "I worked hard for this." She punched his chest with her finger. "It's mine, and no one is gonna take it away from me."

"Come on, sweetheart." Dan started to close the case.

Wanda jerked it away from him. "Pay attention! I told you I'm not going anywhere. But you had better get out of Dodge. I'll take care of the money."

Dan's face flushed with anger. "I thought you loved me. It was just the money all along, wasn't it? How could I have been so stupid?"

Wanda's lip curled. "Listen, you piece of slime! You damned men are all alike. Every one of your brains is in your pants, and yours sure as hell ain't nothing to brag about."

Dan moved toward her. "Now wait a minute."

Wanda slapped him across the face. She screamed at him. "Don't 'now wait a minute' me! Hunter messed up. Then Barnes thought he could fleece me. You're just as expendable. I had to pay them. I just had to pretend I was crazy about you. I don't know which was worse. Understand me. If you open your mouth, you'll be as dead as they are."

Dan's eyes widened as she slipped a gun out of her purse. He realized he was one wrong word from being shot.

Wanda's mouth twisted into a smirk. "That's better. You won't tell anybody anything because if you do, I'll say you planned the whole thing, and I knew nothing about it. Now get out of my fucking way and out of my fucking life! You're so pathetic I'm tempted to kill you, anyway."

She closed the suitcase and sauntered toward the door.

Dan followed her. "Wanda, wait!"

Wanda turned and didn't hesitate. "I told you to keep your mouth shut!" She fired and Dan dropped to the floor.

• • • • • • •

Johnny rushed into the den as Coulter signaled Bannister, who waited outside the house. With a squeal of tires, he blocked Wanda's car in the driveway. Two squad cars arrived for backup. Wanda jumped out of her car and started to run, gripping her gun in one hand and the money in the other.

"Hold it, Wanda," Bannister shouted. His headlights blinded her as she half-turned, aiming at the sound of his voice.

Bannister shot her in the shoulder. She dropped the gun and fell to the ground. He hurried over to her, gun in hand.

"Why didn't you finish me off, flatfoot?"

"I have to admit it was mighty tempting, but I wouldn't dream of cheating the State."

Coulter came back into the den. Dan buried his face in his hands, unable to control his shaking. "She tried to kill me."

Johnny had torn Dan's shirt and tied it around the leg wound. "You're a lucky sombitch," Johnny said. "It's just a flesh wound in your thigh."

Coulter almost felt sorry for Dan. "Well, you carried it off. The three-hundred-thousand is yours when we get it back. Of course, it will be tied up a while as evidence. I guess you earned it."

Johnny handed Coulter one of the tapes. He played part of it back while Johnny admired a video shot of Wanda grabbing the money with the gun in her other hand. They grinned at each other as Coulter put the tapes and video in his briefcase.

"You're in the clear, Dan. We have everything we need," Coulter said. "Come on Johnny, let's get Bannister and wake up Lowell."

44

Coulter could hardly wait for the matron to bring Emily into the visitors' room. His face broke into a broad smile.

Emily's eyes widened as she spied the picnic basket. "You did it!" she cried.

He picked her up and spun her around. "We did it, you and me. Ready to go?"

She looked down. "Do I have to wear this orange jumpsuit?"

"Oh, I almost forgot." He grabbed clothes and sneakers from beside the picnic basket. "Mary sent these. She thought jeans and a sweatshirt would be just right for a picnic."

"Am I really free?"

"You're free as a bird. Hurry and change, then we are getting the hell out of here and heading for the lake."

• • • • •

They lay on a blanket under the huge pecan tree. Emily watched a sailboat drifting in the breeze across the lake. Neither of them had spoken for some time.

Emily finally broke the silence. "I hug trees. My favorite sound is the wind whispering through their leaves."

"For me, it's lake water lapping against the shore. Luckily, we have plenty of both."

Emily took his hand. "I feel like I've been reincarnated, except you have to die first. No. I did die and was reborn. It's the same body, yet I'm not the same person." She looked out at the sailboat. "I've been given a chance to begin a new life, one the old Emily would feel she didn't deserve.

"I can't remember ever being this happy. The trial-by-fire was worth it." She closed her eyes for a moment. "Mary is right. There is no such thing as coincidence. Our paths were there waiting for us, and we each chose to follow where they led."

Coulter kissed her lightly on the mouth. "The important thing is your path led you to me."

EPILOGUE

Downtown Lakewood belonged to a different age. Only a mile from White Rock Lake, the four-block area's street was paved with brick, separate from the parallel city streets of Abrams and Gaston Avenues.

Most of the shops had been there well over half a century. El Chico Restaurant still offered their Tuesday night special enchilada dinner, as they had when they opened some fifty years before.

The Lakewood Café, one of the first buildings, looked ready to fall apart. It was open twenty-four hours a day, served breakfast at any hour, and smokers were welcome. The old Lakewood Theatre still showed vintage movies on weekends and was available for meetings of Lakewood residents.

The entire area said slow down...take your time...relax.

．　．　．　．　．

Coulter's office faced an inner courtyard where he could look out at passersby and shoppers with tired feet resting on the benches. The sign on the courtyard entrance door of Coulter's office said simply, *Attorney.* Most mornings, he joined the old men on the benches, discussing the news of the day and sharing coffee from his huge coffee pot.

Emily and Coulter had divided the space into thirds. Emily's shop encompassed the front of the building. They divided the back in half. One half was his office, and they devoted the other half to her yoga classes and meditation.

Emily's shop was filled with metaphysical books which Mary had helped her choose. Crystals and locally made jewelry filled the display cases. They filled shelves and tables with Tarot Cards, Runes, as well as a large selection of candles, incense, and paraphernalia. Paintings by local artists adorned the white brick walls.

Chairs scattered around the shop invited shoppers to linger. A notice on the large blackboard announced yoga classes on Monday, Wednesday, and Friday from 5:50 to 7:00 p.m. in the open area at the back of the building—or weather permitting—in the courtyard.

• • • • • • •

A boy wearing torn jeans and the remnants of a candy bar on his face peered inside the newly remodeled shop. The sign on the glass front said "*Pathways*". A large black cat sunned himself in the window, while in a nearby satin-lined basket a white, fawn, and chocolate brown Siamese lady and her three kittens napped.

As the boy opened the door, an overhead bell announced his arrival. He saw a young woman look up from arranging some kind of rocks in a display case. Emily's smile was welcoming. She guessed the boy was around ten years old, and he looked troubled.

"Hi. Can I help you?" she asked.

The boy stood on one foot, digging the other into the floor. He finally looked up. "My friend said this is the place where you can talk to a lawyer."

"Your friend was right. My name is Emily. What's yours?"

"Thomas."

"Nice to meet you, Thomas." She pointed to a low swinging gate between two loaded bookcases. "There is the back door to his office. Push the buzzer and he'll open it. I think you'll find him at his desk."

Thomas frowned. "I need some advice, but I never talked to a lawyer before."

"He's pretty easy to talk to. Why don't you go on back? His name's Coulter McBride."

Thomas's face lit up. "Yeah, that's the name. My friend says he works cheap." He hurried to the gate and found the buzzer.

Emily could see them through the open door. Coulter stood up as they shook hands. Thomas dropped into a chair and Coulter took one beside him.

Soon Thomas came back, skipping, and with a wide grin. "Thanks, lady," he called.

"Did everything go okay?"

"Oh, yeah," Thomas said as he hurried out the door.

• • • • •

Emily gazed around her new domain with pride. She sighed with contentment as Coulter slid his arms around her waist. "Were you able to help Thomas?" she asked.

"Interesting case. According to Thomas, the Pound says Rochester can't come home until his fine is paid and Rochester is neutered. Thomas is okay about the money. He knows what neutered means and they aren't doing that to his cat! He wants to hire me to fight it. He says Rochester has rights! I'm going to look into it and see what I can do."

"Ready to go home, Mrs. McBride?" he asked as he kissed her cheek.

She smiled up at him. "Just as soon as I gather up our new family." She picked up the basket holding Godiva and her kittens—two fawn and chocolate, and one little black rascal who was trying to climb out of the basket. Soc followed them outside and Coulter locked the door behind them.

The End

ABOUT THE AUTHOR

Peggy Overbeck is a retired legal assistant, formerly with the litigation department of a Dallas, Texas law firm. She is eighty-five years old, and resides in St. Louis, Missouri, with her cat, Rochester. *The Shaman's Gift* is her debut novel. Peggy's favorite quotes are: "It ain't over, till it's over." – Yogi Berra and "Never give up... never... never... never." –Winston Churchill

NOTE FROM THE AUTHOR

Word-of-mouth is crucial for any author to succeed. If you enjoyed *The Shaman's Gift*, please leave a review online—anywhere you are able. Even if it's just a sentence or two. It would make all the difference and would be very much appreciated.

Thanks!
Peggy Overbeck

We hope you enjoyed reading this title from:

www.blackrosewriting.com

Subscribe to our mailing list – *The Rosevine* – and receive **FREE** books, daily deals, and stay current with news about upcoming releases and our hottest authors.
Scan the QR code below to sign up.

Already a subscriber? Please accept a sincere thank you for being a fan of Black Rose Writing authors.

View other Black Rose Writing titles at
www.blackrosewriting.com/books and use promo code
PRINT to receive a **20% discount** when purchasing.

www.ingramcontent.com/pod-product-compliance
Lightning Source LLC
Chambersburg PA
CBHW010736100726
47899CB00009B/3076